"Everybody Come To The Kitchen. Right Away!"

When Cory, Robert Lee, and Pandora arrived in the kitchen, they saw an empty crisper on the table. "This has gone far enough," Mrs. Dean announced. "Now who ate all the fruit? This is the fourth time I've filled the crisper this week!"

Cory and Robert Lee looked at one another and shook their heads. Then they looked at Pandora.

Pandora edged over toward her nest of towels. She snouted them into position and lay down, head stretched out on the floor. She closed her eyes.

Mrs. Dean looked from the kids to Pandora and back again. "Oh, come on! You're not suggesting . . ."

Books by Joan Carris

Aunt Morbelia and the Screaming Skulls
Just a Little Ham

Available from MINSTREL Books

JUST A LITTLE HAM

JOAN CARRIS

Illustrated by
DORA LEDER

A MINSTREL® BOOK

PUBLISHED BY POCKET BOOKS

New York   London   Toronto   Sydney   Tokyo   Singapore

A Minstrel Book published by
POCKET BOOKS, a division of Simon & Schuster Inc.
1230 Avenue of the Americas, New York, NY 10020

Text copyright © 1989 by Joan Davenport Carris
Illustrations copyright © 1989 by Dora Leder
Front cover illustration by Catherine Huerta

Published by arrangement with
Little Brown & Company Inc.

ISBN: 0-671-74783-5

First Minstrel Books printing April 1993

10 9 8 7 6 5 4 3 2 1

A MINSTREL BOOK and colophon are registered trademarks
of Simon & Schuster Inc.

Printed in the U.S.A.

*I am indebted to Martha McDougald,
who was brave and imaginative
enough to raise a mini-pig in her own
house and who gladly shared her
wealth of information with me.*

For Mindy and the littlest piglet

............JUST A LITTLE HAM

The Piglet Arrives

Cory was almost twelve and her brother Robert Lee
was eight when their mother brought the piglet home.

"Come see what I've got," Mrs. Dean sang out as
she set a cardboard box on the kitchen table.

"Hi, Mom," Cory said as she came into the kitchen.

"Whink?" said the box on the table.

Robert Lee joined them in time to hear the box.
"What's in there?" he asked.

"A fantastic experiment, but probably a pretty fright-
ened one by now," his mother answered. She undid
the box flaps and lifted out the piglet.

It was so small it looked like a toy. It squealed
again — a toy-sized sound more pitiful than the first.

"Poor baby," Cory said, taking it from her mother.
She cradled the pastel pink piglet in her arms.

4

"That's right — keep her warm," Mrs. Dean said. "I'll get her bottles from the car."

"She's ours *to keep?*" Robert Lee cried as his mother dashed out the door.

"No, dopey," Cory said. "People who live in cities don't keep pigs." Actually, Rocky Brook was a large town, not a city, in the middle of New Jersey. And definitely not the right place for a pig, thought Cory.

"Let me hold her," he begged. "Corree! Come on!"

She sighed. Robert Lee Dean appeared to be an angel. With his blond hair, large blue eyes, and innocent smile he had fooled many people, but never his sister. Even though she knew he'd have a fit, she shook her head.

"Wait till she's eaten and isn't so scared."

"I wanta hold her now!" Robert Lee hollered.

"Weeee," squealed the piglet, quivering in Cory's arms.

"Bug-brain! You're scaring her! See how she's shaking?"

Robert Lee frowned but grew quiet as he looked at the piglet. "She is awful little," he said after a bit.

"Probably just born," replied Cory. "Pigs get huge!"

"Not always," their mother said as she came back into the kitchen. She pulled a baby's bottle out of a sack and unscrewed its plastic top to reveal the nipple.

Cory sat at the kitchen table and tried to insert the nipple into the piglet's mouth. After a few drops landed on her tongue, the tiny pig got the idea. She gave one happy grunt and began suckling.

Mrs. Dean tucked an old blue towel around the piglet. "Okay, now we're in business. Robert Lee, come sit on my lap while I explain about this pig."

Robert Lee and his mother settled into the old rocker in the corner of the kitchen. "I said this was a fantastic experiment," she began, "and I meant it. If that little pig lives — and she may not — we're in for a treat."

She could die? Cory stared down at the hungry young thing in her arms. She was an adorable, clean, perfect piglet — more appealing than Cory could ever have imagined.

Cory held her closer. "Why would she die?"

"Because no one knows exactly what to do," Mrs. Dean replied. "She's a week-old orphan who needs a mama pig. I've read everything I could get my hands on today — and so has my staff — but it may not be enough."

"Where'd you get her?" Robert Lee asked.

"From Professor James in the agronomy department. He'd given away her brothers and sisters already. He said he was sure the campus psychologists would want to raise a pig."

Mrs. Dean was herself a psychologist. For the last two years she'd been head of the psychology department of a nearby university. She was Dean Amanda Dean, or Dean Dean.

"Should I burp her like a baby?" Cory asked as she pulled the nipple out of the piglet's mouth.

"EEEEE!" The little pig lunged toward the nipple.

"Keep feeding her," Cory's mom said. "I can't picture a mama pig burping all her piglets. The trick here is to *think* like a pig."

"Oh, hogwash, Mom."

"Hogwash!" Robert Lee repeated. "Get it, Mom?"

"Kids, thinking like a pig is trickier than you believe. Pigs are the smartest of all domestic animals. They can learn anything dogs can learn and much faster. Animal experts rank them right up there with dolphins for intelligence."

An empty-bottle sound filled the kitchen. The piglet stopped sucking on air and poked her snout against Cory's chest. "Weee?" she asked, sounding hopeful. "Weee?"

"She's bein' a pig!" shouted Robert Lee.

Mrs. Dean scooted him off her lap and handed Cory another bottle. "Here. See how much she'll take."

"She'll get sick," Cory warned.

"No she won't," Mrs. Dean said. "A pig rarely overeats — and then only something that's a favorite food. It's a pity so few people know the truth about pigs. We'll learn a lot from this one, you wait and see."

Cory thought, wait a minute, what is this *we* business? The psych department is in charge of this pig. It just can't be another one of Dean Dean's great ideas. Not *this* time.

She remembered the boa constrictor they'd kept so that her mom could study memory in reptiles. It had escaped, to be found days later wrapped around the warm coils of their refrigerator. Gramma had been visiting them at the time, but she went home when the boa constrictor got loose.

Squirrels followed the boa constrictor. They had few traits worth studying, in Cory's opinion. When they began destroying the attic, an exterminator came to evict the whole experiment.

Another time they had taken in Tinka, a Russian girl who spoke no English. They would all learn Russian, Mrs. Dean had said. But no one learned Russian because Tinka ran off with the man who read the gas and electric meters. Cory and Robert Lee rejoiced. Tinka's cooking had been weird.

There had been other animals, plus many depressed or confused students who came to the Deans' house and stayed while they sorted out their lives.

Because of these experiences, Cory was older than her age in years. Gramma said that Cory was loaded with common sense — unlike her mother. She usually felt older than her mother. I look like Mom, Cory thought, grateful that she shared the deep brown hair and blue eyes, but I must be more like Dad.

She had been told everything about her father, whom she could barely remember. He had been a Marine officer in the Middle East, killed while "keeping the peace," the newspaper had said. Cory and

Robert Lee each had a copy of that article in their scrapbooks, along with several pictures. Cory was just under four and Robert Lee was an infant when he died. Robert Lee looked like his dad.

Cory's thoughts were interrupted by her mother. "I'll bet she becomes our all-time favorite house pet."

"*House pet?*" Cory and Robert Lee said together.

"Yes, of course. That's why I brought her home."

The Lap Pig

It was quiet for several seconds in the Deans' kitchen after Mrs. Dean spoke.

Cory thought, I don't believe this.

"Wahoo!" Robert Lee shouted.

Cory frowned at him and turned to her mother. "Mom," she said in her firmest voice, "you can't keep a pig in the house. That's gross! Everybody'll think we're nuts."

"She'll be less trouble than a dog and she's already trained. Pigs are naturally clean. You'll see. As for what everybody thinks, you know my answer on that one."

"She'll get too big, Mom," Cory persisted, looking down at the newly minted pig in her arms. "Even teensy ones like this grow up to be hogs, remember?"

"Not ours. She's a mini-pig. A lap pig. Professor

James promised. He specializes in soil chemistry and livestock and he's a very bright fellow, probably the next head of agronomy. Only a hundred fifty pounds he said, and that's nothing."

Cory tried to imagine how she at seventy-five pounds would hold a pig twice that size on her lap. While she watched, the second bottle went empty. Only 150 pounds, huh? By *next week* if she keeps eating like this.

The piglet let go of the nipple. She grunted and yawned pinkly against Cory's chest. "Wrunk, wrunk," she murmured in contentment as she burrowed into the towel.

"I know just what she's sayin'!" Robert Lee exclaimed.

"That's what Professor James told me. He said we'd always know how she felt by the sounds she made and what she did." Mrs. Dean paused, and then she giggled. "Can't you just imagine what Momma and Poppa Dean would say if they knew we were raising a pig in the house?"

Robert Lee hooted at the idea.

Cory knew exactly what her father's parents would say. They ran a large family farm in Kentucky. Poppa Dean was especially proud of his hogs.

"Ham what am," he was fond of saying as they sat down to Sunday dinner. "You poor city folk from New Jersey have to come to Kentucky to get real food."

Yup, pig equals ham, Cory thought.

Just then the piglet snorted in her sleep, wormed deeper into Cory's arms, and began to snore softly.

Cory smiled in spite of herself. Such an incredibly tiny, helpless thing . . . contented now. Cory could feel it.

"You know, Gramma's coming in a couple months," Cory said, aware that her mother was thinking only of her new experiment. "And she hated the boa constrictor and the squirrels."

"Oh, but a pig is different," Mrs. Dean said airily. "Anyway, Gramma's tried all my life to turn me into a normal person who does what's expected, and she's given up now. She loves me anyway — flaky but happy." She smiled.

"Right," Cory said. "I wondered if you knew."

"Oh, I know. It's a good thing I have a healthy ego. Anyway, I'll set up the playpen now. I have chopped straw, too, for the litter pan, and towels for bedding."

"I should probably go do my homework," Cory said, wishing she could forget homework for once. Or do it quickly without caring so much, like her friend Willa.

Cory knew she was more grown up than most of the kids in her class. Willa and Hope often teased her, saying, "Yes, Mother dear," when she'd said something particularly adult. Cory would sigh and know that she had goofed again. She was waiting for college when everyone would be grown up.

"No homework yet," her mom was saying. "We have

to hold her." She tapped her head. "Think like a pig, remember? We are the mama pig now, and we are this baby's security."

"It's my turn anyway," said Robert Lee, stretching out eager arms. "I can watch TV and hold her till dinner."

"You two think of a good name while I set up the playpen and an electric heater to keep her warm," said their mother.

Robert Lee held the piglet tenderly. He gazed down at her and said, "She's so beautiful. I didn't know a pig was beautiful. And she likes how I hold her. See?"

Cory saw several things — how gentle he was being and how patient he had been waiting for his turn. He hadn't whined once. Maybe her mother wasn't totally flaky. Robert Lee needed to think about something other than himself. He had been spoiled by too many people for too long.

"She really likes you, I can tell," Cory said. "An animal always knows whether people are kind or mean. She can tell you love her."

Robert Lee beamed. "We oughta name her Petunia . . . or Popsicle — something that begins with a 'P' to go with pig."

"Well, maybe," she said, stalling for time. She had been thinking of Victoria or Elizabeth or Mehitabel — unusual names for a pig. Her eyes fell on her English book and she remembered a story from Greek mythology.

"How about Pandora?" she asked. She was never going to tell him that Pandora had caused endless trouble in the story. But she knew she had hit on the perfect name.

"Yeah! Pandora Pig," Robert Lee crooned, all unknowing.

· One thing Cory's mother had failed to say was how often Pandora would eat. The Deans were in the middle of dinner when a demanding "WEEE!" came from the playpen.

Pandora had left her nest of towels. Now she stood on her hind legs, tiny snout poking at the playpen netting, eyes fixed on the family at the table. "WEEEE!" she shrilled again. There was no mistaking her meaning.

"Isn't she a smart one?" Mrs. Dean said.

"Isn't she cute?" cooed Robert Lee.

"Isn't she loud!" Cory said. "And it's only been three hours since she ate. But you can tell she's hungry."

"WEEEE! WEEEE! WEEEE!"

Mrs. Dean said, "Luckily Professor James gave me a supply of bottles. They're in the fridge now, so we'll have to warm one."

Pandora cried "WEEEE!" until the nipple was in her mouth.

"Who's going to feed her during the night?" Cory asked as the milk in the bottle dwindled rapidly. If I have to get up every few hours, she thought, and warm bottles in the middle of the night . . .

"They're not supposed to eat quite this often," Mrs. Dean said as she began clearing the table.

Just then Cory heard the flap-flap of the pet door in the laundry room next to the kitchen. The family cats strolled in — the tabby Rain first, followed by Drizzle, daughter of Rain.

Both stopped short in the doorway. Rain's whiskers twitched and her ears flattened. Drizzle, a lighter gray tabby than her mother, hissed and arched her back.

Cory had an inspiration. "Here, Robert Lee, you can feed her if you want. I'll fix the cats' dinner. They're jealous already."

While Cory fixed their food, Rain and Drizzle stalked around the kitchen on suspicious paws. They inspected the piglet, the playpen, the towel nest, and the new litter pan. Their tails switched and kept right on switching as they ate hastily, often looking back over their shoulders. Then they hid under the living room sofa.

Cory tried to coax them out to explain about Pandora. Rain and Drizzle glared at her and would have no part of it. When Pandora shrilled "WEEE!" for her second bottle, they retreated even farther under the sofa.

Finally Cory gave up coaxing. She was afraid that cats and pigs didn't make friends. Poor Rain and Drizzle. They would never understand.

Robert Lee fell asleep in the rocker with Pandora in his lap.

Later, homework finished, Cory came into the kitchen and found her mother looking down on the sleeping pair. "This is a picture you don't see very often," her mom said. "Aren't they adorable?"

"Yes, when they're asleep," Cory agreed, smiling.

"I'll tuck them in bed. Don't worry about Pandora at night, honey. I'll feed her, and soon she'll eat enough during the day that she'll sleep nights just like any baby."

Uh-huh, Cory thought. Maybe. And maybe not.

· Pandora called for food at eleven that evening and again at three A.M. Seven o'clock in the morning found Mrs. Dean in the rocker with her again when Cory came downstairs.

"She's waiting four hours now, as Professor James said she would. We'll go to the vet this afternoon as soon as I get home. Can you feed her at lunch?"

"Sure, but I can't get home again till almost four."

"Honey, this is going to be so exciting!" Mrs. Dean's enthusiasm filled the kitchen. "Soon we can teach her to come to her name, to fetch, to run races —"

"Run races? A pig?"

"Oh yes! In England they've trained bird pigs who point and retrieve as well as dogs. There are guard pigs, too — better than dogs. They sleep less on the job.

Also . . . and I just now thought of this . . . you can probably make money from her this summer."

Mrs. Dean's last remark was lost on Cory, who was imagining Pandora guarding their house and yard — waddling along the fence and grunting at passersby. On their fence would be a sign that read BEWARE! VICIOUS PIG.

"Oh, Mom!"

"I'm serious! By May — in just a month — we'll take her jogging to keep her in peak condition. There's an Arizona study . . . Well, I can read that to you later."

Cory's mind flashed a picture of a pig in jogging sweats and running shoes. And then, minds being unpredictable as they are, she thought of her Gramma, who often wore fleecy sweatsuits. Had Gramma heard any of these wacko ideas?

"Mom, have you talked to Gramma lately?"

"Yes, after you were in bed." Mrs. Dean removed one bottle from Pandora's mouth and inserted a second.

"Well?"

"She told me I had lost the few marbles that I had."

Cory chuckled. That was Gramma, all right. Except . . . what if other people felt the same way? What would her friends Hope and Willa think? Worse yet, what about Andy Barton, who teased her every time he had a chance? Just thinking about what *he* would say made Cory groan out loud.

Her classmates had always lived in the city. They thought of pigs as dirty, smelly farm animals wallowing in mud. And if they saw her jogging with Pandora . . . ? Well, it was too much. If *only* her mother could be normal — like other mothers.

Still, here was Pandora-the-Spotless in her very own house, using a litter pan like a tidy house cat. *Somebody* was very confused about pigs, Cory decided.

Pandora versus the Vet

At school that morning, Cory told Hope and Willa about her mom's newest experiment. "You have to keep this a secret," she begged. "This whole idea's nuts."

Not to Hope it wasn't. She pleaded to see the piglet that day. Hope, a small, fair girl with gray-blue eyes, was an easy victory for Pandora.

"She's so cute I can't stand it!" Hope cried the second she saw her. She held Pandora while Cory frantically warmed bottles. Guess I needn't have worried what *she* would think, Cory decided.

"WEEEE!"

"She's got no patience at all," Cory said. "Have you ever heard so much noise?"

Pandora didn't stop crying until the nipple was in her mouth.

"Can I give her the next bottle?" Hope asked.

"Sure. Mom's bringing home bigger bottles today, but when they're gone we have to start making the formula ourselves." Cory shook her head. "She's cute, but I'll bet she's going to be a lot of work."

Hope nodded. "That's how babies are. I think they're wonderful." Hope was the busiest baby-sitter in the neighborhood. Her goal in life, since kindergarten, had been to have six children. She was herself an only child.

Now she said, "Maybe I'll have eight or nine instead of just six."

"Eight or nine kids? We won't tell Willa, okay?" Cory grinned at Hope.

Their friend Willa, who sang in the school chorus with them, was now at soccer practice. She was coming after dinner to see Pandora. For years, she and Cory had been suggesting great careers to Hope.

"You could be a stewardess and go all over the world," they had told her. "Or a lawyer like that cool girl on TV. Or a famous singer — how about that?"

Hope was never interested. But let a woman pass them with a stroller and Hope turned on. "Did you see him?" she would drool after the baby had been wheeled past. "All that fuzzy hair and those teeny-tiny tennis shoes? I should've asked his mom if she needed a sitter."

"WEEEE!" shrilled Pandora, looking for the next bottle.

Hope swiftly traded places with Cory. When she held the suckling piglet in her arms she said, "I can do this every afternoon, okay? If I don't have a sitting job."

Cory's first thought was, okay by me. Most afternoons Robert Lee wouldn't be at Scouts and he could feed her. He'd probably want early evenings, too.

That left only the lunchtime feedings for Cory. Hey, wait a minute, she thought. Mom said she'll grow fast. Pretty soon she won't take a bottle. Pretty soon no more baby pig. Somehow, Cory knew she'd miss that baby.

"We'll see," Cory said finally, not wanting to hurt Hope's feelings. "Do you want to go to the vet with us? Mom will be here soon. Why don't you call home and ask?"

By four-thirty that afternoon Mrs. Dean, the girls, and the piglet were in the car. Cory sat up front holding Pandora, asleep in her blue towel. When the motor came on, Pandora woke up. "Whink?" She squirmed up out of her towel and looked around as they backed out the driveway.

Hope leaned over the seat to watch. "Is she afraid of riding in the car?"

Pandora was not afraid. She wormed out of her towel until her front hooves were resting on the window ledge. Eagerly she peered out the window as trees and houses and cars went by. "Whink!" she squeaked with delight.

Cory grinned at the little face so close to her own.

"This's the cutest thing I ever saw . . ." Hope began.

Just then an approaching car passed them and swerved wildly as the driver craned his head to look back.

"Uh oh," said Mrs. Dean. "I think our pig is a traffic hazard."

"A real road hog," Cory joked.

Pandora's snout pressed against the window. Every now and then she gave another joyous "Whink!" and bounced her back hooves against Cory.

Drivers and passengers in nearby cars all noticed the pig. Cory had never seen so many astounded, disbelieving faces. She felt odder by the minute. I wish Mom cared what other people think — *just once*, she fumed.

By the time they arrived at the vet's office, they had barely missed being rammed by several cars. In the vet's driveway, a van veered toward them.

"Idiot! Haven't you ever seen a pig before?" Mrs. Dean shouted at the woman driving the van.

Pandora sat on Cory's lap in the waiting room. Her snout tested the air. Like antennae, her tiny ears turned toward each plaintive bark or mournful meow.

"Wee," she whimpered when she made up her mind. She thrust her head under Cory's arm and lay very still.

Cory felt Pandora's misery. She looked over at her mother, who was studying the piglet with a professional eye.

"Mom," Cory said, *"she knows*. How can she know?"

"Well, animals do sense fear in other animals. She can smell disinfectant and medicines, too, and they're strange. Pigs have a very keen sense of smell. In France they hunt for fungi called truffles. A good sow can smell a truffle twenty feet away — and that truffle is a foot underground. Isn't that amazing?"

"She smells trouble," Hope concluded.

"Dean?" came a deep, melodious voice from the entryway to the examining rooms. It was Dr. Samuel Tilden, known as Dr. Sam. He was a slender, spectacled black man with an unforgettable voice and manner. He sang in concerts throughout New Jersey, and all of his patients had his home number in case of an emergency.

Cory loved Dr. Sam. Whenever Rain or Drizzle had to visit the vet, Cory came along. Today, knowing he would be intrigued, she held up the piglet and said, "Surprise!"

"Ahh, *sus domesticus*," he said with a twinkle. "Another experiment?"

Mrs. Dean rose. "Actually, this one's a house pet. But Professor James from the agronomy department says that pigs get many diseases, so she needs her shots."

All eyes in the waiting room were on them. Terrific, Cory thought glumly. My mother, the Town Crier.

Dr. Sam said, "Come on back and we'll talk."

Once they were all in the small examination room, Dr. Sam took Pandora from Cory's arms. "Weee," she squealed, poking her head inside his white coat.

The veterinarian sat down with her on the low examining table. "She's extremely tiny," he began.

Mrs. Dean interrupted. "She's a mini-pig, not a regular pig, Dr. Sam."

He held the piglet up for a longer look. "That's good. I thought you had a runt here. I was all set to give my never-pick-a-runt speech." He chuckled, then fell silent.

"In the house?" he asked, after he'd felt the piglet all over. "You really want her in the house?"

"We'll all learn much more that way," Mrs. Dean said.

"Oh, there's no doubt about that," he replied.

Cory thought, uh-huh. He thinks we're crazy.

"Well, now," the vet continued, "you must set aside a part of the yard where she can root in clean dirt and grass — the cleaner the better. There's an old saying, 'Root or die,' and it's the truth. Pigs get vital minerals, especially iron, from rooting."

"No problem," Mrs. Dean said. "Our yard has plenty of space, front and back."

Not in the front, Mom! Cory prayed silently. If Andy Barton knew she had a pig as a front-lawn ornament, he would never let up. Cory shuddered. Still, Dr. Sam had calmly accepted Pandora as their pet. He was jabbering away as if pigs in town were normal.

"Let her root in one section for a few months, then give her a clean section."

As Cory, her mother, and Hope listened, he continued with suggestions and information. Gradually, Cory was caught up in the idea in spite of her misgivings. Like her mother, Dr. Sam believed that Pandora would be an amusing, exciting pet. And Cory trusted him completely.

While he was visiting with them, Dr. Sam filled a syringe for Pandora's first immunization.

"There we go," he said, inserting the needle into the piglet's neck.

"WEEE!" shrieked Pandora, oozing out of his hands. She launched herself off the table and landed on the floor, where she squealed wildly and tried to gain a footing on the shiny surface.

Dr. Sam slammed the door shut.

"WEEE!" she shrilled. She turned, hooves slipping. "WEEE! WEEE! WEEE!"

Cory wanted to laugh and cry at the same time. With the piglet's feet splayed out from under her, she looked like a cartoon pig on ice. But she was terrified, and that wasn't funny.

"WEEE!"

"I've got her!"

"WEEEEEE!"

"You get her!"

"WEEEEE!"

"Poor thing!" That was Hope and Cory together. "WEEEEEEEE! WEEEEEEEE!"

Cory grabbed one hind leg and held on. She stuffed Pandora up under her jacket and held her tight so that

she'd feel safe. "Her heart's thumping like mad," Cory said.

Dr. Sam, Hope, and Mrs. Dean sagged against the walls.

Mrs. Dean spoke first. "I don't want her traumatized at such a young age."

"Nor do I want a trauma at my advanced age," said Dr. Sam. "We'll try a different approach. Cory, you sit on the stool and hold her. I'll sweet-talk her a bit."

For several minutes, Dr. Sam stroked Pandora and rubbed behind her ears. Softly he began to sing to the tune of "Oh What a Beautiful Mornin'."

> *Oh what a beautiful pig-let,*
> *oh what a glorious pig . . .*

"Wrunk."

"Keep singing," Cory whispered.

> *We know a most charming pig-let,*
> *she'll be the sow of our dreams . . .*

"Wrunk, wrunk."

Dr. Sam sighed. "I'm sorry. She needs another shot. They aren't painful, but pigs loathe shots."

"We believe you," replied Mrs. Dean. "Cory will hold on and you do what you have to do."

Cory hated the next minute as much as Pandora. The tiny animal shrieked nonstop — piercing, high-pitched cries that brought everyone in the clinic to their doorway.

When it was over, the vet's glasses were askew and he was breathing heavily. "You'd think we were drawing and quartering her alive," he said. "Nobody hates the vet as much as a smart pig."

He turned to Mrs. Dean. "At least you'll have her manure for gardening. That's some reward."

"Yes. I have a plan for it, too. Well, thanks for everything, Dr. Sam. I'll read all of the pamphlets you've given us, and we'll return on schedule for her other shots."

Cory closed her eyes. *Other shots.* Those were the two worst words she had heard in years.

Back in the car, Pandora immediately put her mini-hooves on the window ledge. "Whink!" she piped gleefully as they turned onto the street.

"Hmmph!" Cory sniffed, half relieved and half annoyed. "That was all an act back there. You're just a little ham!"

Hog Heaven

Mrs. Dean and Cory dropped Hope off at her house
after their trip to the vet. Hope dragged her mother
out to the car to admire Pandora, the very thing Cory
had been dreading.

"It really *is* a pig," Mrs. Langley said, as though
needing to convince herself. "She's darling . . . but
Amanda, are you sure you know what you're doing?
Hope tells me you have her in the house."

"In the kids' old playpen. And no, we don't know
exactly what we're doing. We plan to learn as we go.
It should be fascinating."

"I imagine so." Hope's mother smiled faintly.
"Come on, Hope. I need you to put on a fresh tablecloth. Bye!"

Pandora squealed happily as the car picked up speed.

And again, other drivers gawked at the tiny pig and nearly lost control of their cars. Avoiding them took Mrs. Dean's full attention. Even so, she was muttering something.

"What's that, Mom?"

"Fresh tablecloth, my eye! The day I start worrying about tablecloths . . ."

"Now, Mom," said Cory, trying to soothe her. "Mrs. Langley doesn't have anything else to do."

"Well, she could have!" Mrs. Dean retorted. "Whenever I run across people like that I think of what Eden Phillpotts said: 'The universe is full of magical things patiently waiting for our wits to grow sharper.' "

Here Mrs. Dean waved one hand in the air. "So why isn't she out here looking for those magical things? They're all around us!" She pointed at Pandora. "We have one in the car and she didn't even know or care!"

That's true, Cory thought, thinking of what she had learned from Pandora already. But she didn't say anything. When her mom got on the topic of being useful to society or curious about life, it was better to let her get it out of her system. When she said, "A mind is a terrible thing to waste," the speech would be over.

As they entered the back door, Mrs. Dean said, "You know, Cory, a mind is *truly* a terrible thing to waste!"

Cory grinned. "Hey, Mom, what's for dinner?"

"Dinner? Well, we have a lot of pig formula . . ."

Luckily, the Deans also had the makings for a giant taco salad, one of their favorite meals. After dinner was over, Cory crawled partway under the couch — into the dark with Rain and Drizzle. She knew their feelings were hurt. She usually knew how others around her felt. Her mom said she was "a natural psychologist."

"But I'm not going to *be* one," Cory would reply firmly. Her mom had said that nothing was definite in psychology. "We don't have perfect answers," she'd told Cory.

Yet Cory loved definite, perfect answers — at the end of a math problem or in science lab, for instance. She could hardly wait for more math and chemistry in high school.

Now, half under the couch, half out, Cory lay on her stomach and talked to the cats until Willa came. Willa was tall, with black hair in a heavy braid down her back. She looked strong, unlike Hope, who appeared rather fragile.

When Willa arrived, Robert Lee was proudly in charge of Pandora. "She burps sometimes," he explained as he set the piglet upright in his lap.

Pandora belched on cue.

"Can I hold her?" Willa pleaded.

It was dumb to worry, all right, Cory decided as she watched Willa and Pandora settle into the rocker. Hope and Willa are crazy about her.

Robert Lee scowled nearby. "I didn't get to hold her all afternoon," he said.

"You can help give her her bath," said his mother. "Let her sleep a bit first while you and I make a fuss over Rain and Drizzle. They're still sulking under the couch."

Pandora snored contentedly in Willa's lap while the girls talked. "I got my camp stuff today," Willa said. "We do sports all morning and music in the afternoon. Mornings sound great, but I don't know about blowing into that flute for hours." She made a face.

Willa's mother expected her to be a musician, a famous flutist. Her father hoped she would earn a soccer scholarship to college. Willa wasn't sure what she wanted. She often asked Cory's mother, "What if I don't *want* to keep playing soccer or be a flutist when I grow up?"

Mrs. Dean reassured her each time. "Willa, listen to your heart. You're a smart girl. You will know what's right for you when the time comes."

Cory had always believed her mom's advice, basically, but she wasn't going to sit around waiting for a magic answer. Poppa Dean once told her about the different summer jobs her own father had had as a boy. "Learned all kinds of things. Full of drive, that boy," Poppa Dean had bragged, pride mixed with grief in his voice.

Cory wanted jobs, too, just like her dad. That way she'd know what work she liked and what she didn't.

"I'm not going to Momma and Poppa Dean's in Kentucky this summer," she told Willa. "I'm taking diving lessons and I want a real job."

"Will people hire twelve-year-olds?" Willa asked, knowing Cory would be twelve in July.

"Some jobs, yeah. Mothers' helpers and yard stuff. Maybe a newspaper route."

"Barf."

"I know, but Hope'll make tons of money as a mother's helper. She's taking diving lessons with me every morning, but that won't fill up the whole summer."

The girls talked and Pandora napped. After a time she woke up with a snort. She stretched her hind legs out behind and her front legs forward. Cory took her from Willa and put her in the playpen.

Pandora trotted straight to her straw litter and did her business. She galloped three teeny gallops across the width of the playpen and stood up, hooves in the netting. "Wee?" she asked, eyes on Cory. "Weee?"

"My folks have to see this," marveled Willa. "She's too much! I wish I had a pig . . . except, that stuff stinks. Pew!"

"It's gross, isn't it? We take it out right away to a place Mom fixed for it. I'll be right back."

When she returned, Pandora was still standing up and begging, so Cory picked her up. "She wants to be held all the time." Cory looked down into the tiny face. "I think she's smiling — and she's only nine days old!"

The girls collected Robert Lee from the living room and they all went upstairs to the bathroom. The Deans' bath was the most modern room in the house, with a large, sunken tub under an oval skylight.

"Be sure she doesn't get chilled," Mrs. Dean called after them. "Keep the heater on for the whole time."

Robert Lee ran the bath, taking forever to get the temperature right. At last he put Pandora on all four feet into the tub. "Oooh, nice bath," he cooed, sprinkling warm drops on Pandora's head and snout.

Pandora didn't need a sales pitch. She licked the drops of water off her snout and went "Whink!" She trotted the length of the tub, turned, and trotted back toward the faucets. Trit, trot, trit, trot, trit, trot.

Then she stopped in the middle of the tub. Splash, splash! with her front hooves. Splash, splash! with the back ones. "WHINK!" she trumpeted, glorying in the water.

"Just like a kid in a mud puddle," Willa said. "Do you think I could call my folks to come over now? And Hope, too. She'll go bananas."

Talk about an instant success! Cory thought. She could imagine the newspaper headline: PRECIOUS PIGLET WOWS THEM IN ROCKY BROOK. Still, her mom had warned her and Robert Lee about too many people too soon. "One guest at a time," she had said.

Cory explained this to Willa while Pandora cavorted in the tub. She lay down and blew bubbles with her snout. She rolled over and over, the length of the tub.

Robert Lee loved the show. He ran warmer water to keep up the temperature and Pandora stood under the running faucet. "WHEEENK!" This was more fun than anything else.

"That pig talks!" Willa said.

"Does she ever," agreed Cory, remembering the trip to the vet. She glanced around the waterlogged bathroom. "Hey, Robert Lee, this is making a mess."

"She can't help it. She's a baby," he said. "More shower, Pandora?" he offered.

Good idea, Cory thought. We'll turn on the shower in the tub when she's bigger. What she could do as a full-grown pig in a regular bath . . . Now that would be *some headline*.

After half an hour, Mrs. Dean insisted on putting Robert Lee to bed. "Cory, dry Pandora off now. It's getting late."

· The rest of April went much the same way — Pandora's way. Though her body was tiny, her will was enormous.

As days went by, she grew skilled at looking and sounding pathetic when she wanted something. "Wee-eeee," she would cry soulfully. When that didn't work, she screamed. She also learned that Robert Lee was her slave.

"She's in hog heaven here," Mrs. Dean said one Saturday evening as she held the sleeping piglet. "I told Professor James how well she has adjusted to being a pet."

In fact, everyone in the house had adjusted. Cory was curled up reading on the couch with Rain and Drizzle beside her. Rain had decided to ignore Pandora.

Drizzle stalked her whenever the piglet had the run of the kitchen. If Drizzle came too close, Pandora thrust out her snout and went "Oink!" in the cat's face. Drizzle would then sit down to groom herself, as though the piglet weren't there.

Now Cory said, "It's heaven, Mom, because she always gets what she wants. But she weighed twenty-five pounds this morning. What'll we do when she gets big and does just what she wants?"

Of them all, Cory understood Pandora the best. She knew when the piglet was being stubborn, like Robert Lee. She knew the meaning of each cry or grunt, each sound of joy, puzzlement, or anger. Pandora was fascinating, even if she was spoiled. Still, Cory could foresee trouble.

"You're absolutely right, dear. Tomorrow we'll put a harness on her, and a leash after a few days. She must begin to mind us, even though she may not like it."

Cory chuckled. "Oh, she won't like it."

Nor did she. She hated the rose red leather harness. She tried to work it off by rubbing vigorously against the table legs in the kitchen. "Oink!" she grunted as she rubbed. The table shook as Pandora rubbed and oinked.

Mrs. Dean frowned. Robert Lee protested. Cory said, "Hey, if we give in on this, it's all over!"

"You're right, Cory . . . as always," her mother said. "We'll just ignore her. Let's go outside and work on her pen. She needs to be rooting for those tasty minerals."

Pandora also hated the matching, rose red leather leash. She didn't want it trailing after her and she especially didn't want anyone on the other end of it.

Robert Lee tried to take her for a walk in the house. Pandora sat down. She glued her bottom to the floor and yelled, "EEEE!" as long as Robert Lee tugged on the leash.

"She won't go!" he hollered over her piercing cries.

"Don't jerk the leash. Pull steady!" Cory called out.

"Everybody hush!" When it was quiet Mrs. Dean said, "No one ever trained an animal by yelling, Robert Lee. The minute you yell, you have lost control. Is that clear?"

Robert Lee stomped his foot.

"Temper won't work either. Now, think. What would make you want to go on a leash?"

"Nothing," he replied honestly.

Cory asked herself, what makes a person want to do something? Something hard or scary or different? Instantly, she imagined the diving board. The idea of going off head first was really scary. But she wanted to be a good diver. She wanted her friends to say, "Oh, Cory, what a great dive!" That would be her reward.

"A reward," Cory said out loud. "We have to bribe her."

Robert Lee's face lit up. "Peanut butter!" he shouted.

"WEEE!" scolded Pandora, who hated loud voices. She could yell whenever she felt like it, but no one else was supposed to.

"Brilliant, Robert Lee," Cory said. All month they had buried Pandora's vitamins and cod liver oil pills in balls of peanut butter. It was the only way she would take them.

Now, walking over to Robert Lee, Cory wafted a new and larger ball of peanut butter under Pandora's snout. "Here it is, Pandora. You have to come here to get it."

It took two days before Pandora relented. And then she would only cross the kitchen on her leash before she sat down and opened her mouth. Eventually, grumbling all the way, she condescended to trot around the yard.

Cory tried to leave the house with her on the leash one afternoon at the very end of April. Snout quivering,

Pandora parked herself in the doorway. "Oink!" she grunted as she sniffed Cory.

At first Cory couldn't imagine what was wrong. Then she knew. As soon as she'd wrapped a ball of peanut butter in a piece of bread, she picked up the leash again. "Ready, Madam?" she asked.

"Wrunk." Pandora rose to her feet.

"I can see who's training who," Cory muttered. "Just remember, Pandora, nobody likes a smarty-pig."

Later, laughing, she told her mother what Pandora had done. "I'm taking her to school next week," Cory went on, "and I'm giving a talk about pigs for extra credit. But nobody's going to believe me!"

"Cory, I'm so pleased!" crowed Mrs. Dean. "And you won't be sorry, I just know it. Everyone who sees her falls in love with her. And if they don't believe the facts, that's their tough luck." She closed the book she'd been reading. "By the way . . . are you and Robert Lee remembering to stir our lovely compost every day?"

"Yes, but I wouldn't call it lovely."

"Well I would. You'll earn lovely money this summer from that mixture of straw and manure."

"You've got to be kidding!"

Mrs. Dean shook her head. "No, I'm not. You can sell bags of our composted straw and manure. City people are just dying for the real thing — or so Professor James keeps telling me. You'll see."

Oh no, Cory thought. I won't do it. I can't do it. She saw herself pulling Robert Lee's red wagon. In the wagon were bags of the real thing.

"No way, Mom!" she said. "I'm not spending the summer like that. I won't be president of Pig Poop, Incorporated!"

Pandora Goes
to School

When she saw they were getting into the car, Pandora became so excited she nearly jumped out of Cory's arms.

"Whink! Whink!" she squealed as Mrs. Dean revved the motor.

"Perfect memory," Cory's mom remarked. "It's been a month since she rode in the car, but she remembers."

She turned to Cory. "You have your speech? And you're sure Robert Lee's principal will bring you home after you're finished at the grade school?"

"Yes. Ouch! Pandora!" Cory flinched as the piglet's back hooves dug through her slacks and into her legs. Pandora was again peering out the window, her front hooves on its sill, her snout testing the fresh May breeze. She jumped for joy and Cory was her trampoline.

"I'll bet those hooves hurt, don't they? Here, use this." Mrs. Dean took the small pillow she kept as a back support while driving and stuck it in Cory's lap.

Just be cool, Cory told herself as Pandora jounced up and down. She was praying for an "A" on her talk in science class. She had gotten a "B+" on the last big science test, though, and maybe . . . maybe, that boo-boo could cost her the "A" she counted on for her report card.

Mrs. Dean dropped her and Pandora off at Rocky Brook Junior High, home to the sixth, seventh, and eighth grades. Cory hid in the girls' bathroom with Pandora, just as she and Miss Huffberger, the science teacher, had planned.

I am *not* nervous, Cory told herself. Some kids already know we have a pig for a pet, so no big deal. Except there's Andy Barton. He hasn't said a word, so he must not know. Why couldn't he be in the *other* sixth-grade class?

At 8:35 exactly Cory stood outside the classroom door, Pandora a heavy weight in her arms. She listened, and there came the cue.

"What farm animal," Miss Huffberger was asking the class, "is thought of as being fat and muddy and lazy?"

"The pig!" chorused the students.

Cory nudged the door open and let Pandora go. Delighted as always to run free, the piglet romped around the edge of the room. "Whink?" she asked, stopping to test one boy's shoe with her sensitive snout. She squealed softly, trotting from place to place.

"Hi, Pandora," Hope and Willa said in turn. They were the only ones who rubbed behind Pandora's ears, and so she stayed longer by them.

Miss Huffberger, tall and thin and deadly serious on most days, was today all smiles. She bent over and picked up Pandora. "WEEE!" the piglet complained.

"Awww, isn't it cute?" cried several girls. "Just like Hope and Willa said."

"Look at its little, squiggly tail!"

"Listen to it yell!" Giggle, giggle.

Cory came forward before Pandora decided to get really mad. "We could just let her run around," she told Miss Huffberger. "Then everyone could pet her while I talk."

"EEEEEE!" squealed Pandora, struggling to escape.

"I think she agrees with you," Miss Huffberger said, bending over to put Pandora on the floor.

While Pandora snorkeled her way around the room, Miss Huffberger inspected her clothes. "Well," she said, "there's certainly no mud. Cory, why don't you tell us about pigs?"

"Yeah, Cory, we just can't wait," came a loud stage whisper from the first row.

"That will be quite enough, Andrew," said the teacher.

I knew it, Cory thought. She refused to even look at him. She didn't have to. She had seen the impish

grin and the dark, all-seeing eyes of Andy Barton for years. This time, she smiled and told herself again to be cool.

Hope and Willa smiled back from the third row, and Cory began.

"I used to think pigs were dirty and smelly, just like everybody does, until we got Pandora. She's an orphan, so she might have died if we hadn't taken her in."

Andy began humming the death march.

"Shut up," ordered Tab Carter, kicking Andy in the foot. "Are there any more little pigs?" he asked Cory.

Miss Huffberger glared at both boys and shook a warning finger.

Cory went on. "This is a miniature pig, called a mini-pig. She'll be only a hundred fifty pounds or so when she's grown up. Regular pigs can be over a thousand pounds, and one old boar — that's a male pig — was nearly two thousand pounds.

"Pigs grow very fast. Pandora is called a shoat now, but she'll be a gilt when she's grown up at six months. After she's a mother she'll be called a sow. At five weeks she weighs twenty-seven pounds, which is getting to be kind of heavy to lug around."

Cory explained how they had bottle-fed Pandora every four hours at first. She described Pandora's playpen and the straw-litter routine. "She's never made a mistake," Cory said. "Dogs are lots harder to train. Pigs hate messes where they live."

Andy's sharp eyes surveyed the boys, sparking a chorus of male snorting.

"It's true!" Cory said, blue fire in her eyes. "Her favorite thing is a bath. She gets one every night after dinner. When we run water in the kitchen now, she begs to get up in the sink."

Cory felt as if she were swimming upstream against a strong current, but she plowed on. She told how grown pigs made excellent watchdogs, how pigs in Europe dug for truffles and acted as birdhogs. She listed the ways pigs had contributed to medical science — all the information Mrs. Dean had learned from her reading.

By the time she finished, every kid had petted Pandora. They saw how clean she was and how friendly — how she sniffed everything with her snout, bouncing from one luscious smell to another. And still they had questions.

"Watchhogs? That's dumb. Pigs just sleep and eat!"

"They do not!" said Hope.

"Pigs don't hunt birds, they eat 'em. Heh, heh," Andy sniggered.

"Blow it out your ear!" snapped Willa.

"This is the only clean pig I've ever seen. If they hate dirt, why're they always so muddy?"

Questions flew at Cory like angry stones.

Miss Huffberger held up her hand for silence. "Most people," she said, "have fixed ideas about pigs that they refuse to change — even when the evidence says otherwise."

Grimly, she went on. "Now that's called prejudice. It's the opposite of intelligence and it reveals a closed mind. *No one with a closed mind can ever become a scientist.* Do you *want* to be people with closed minds — with prejudices?"

Subdued, most students shook their heads no. The more stubborn ones exchanged meaningful glances.

"All right, Cory," Miss Huffberger said, "now to the questions. First, why are pigs usually seen as dirty animals?"

Cory spoke quickly. "Because they don't have a chance to wash every day — or lots of times a day. Pandora would if she could. Mom says she'll die this summer if she gets toc 'ot. Pigs'll do anything to cool off, so they roll in mud or whatever's wet. Mud acts like suntan lotion for them because pigs can get bad sunburns."

"And the watchhogs?" prompted the teacher.

Cory grinned. "Mom made a copy of this article and picture to pass around. I forgot it before." She handed the clipping to Tab Carter in the front row.

"That sow is guarding a farmer's barn," she explained. "The farmer said she would attack, too. Once she chased his tractor when it got too close to her piglets. You can read the part where he says she hardly ever sleeps when she's on guard, but his dog sleeps all the time."

"Now the birdhogs," said Miss Huffberger.

Cory shrugged. "I haven't seen any pictures, but it makes sense. Pigs have awesome snouts. It's their best thing. So why wouldn't they be better than dogs at smelling birds?" She hesitated. "Except . . . they're really hard to train. It took us forever to make Pandora go for a walk on her leash. Maybe people just don't know how to train pigs."

"Exactly," agreed Miss Huffberger. "Still, pigs are thought to be the only domesticated animals that can actually solve problems. In scientific tests, a grown pig faced with a new problem can devise an original solution — a way out of the problem. And that, people, is the definition of intelligence."

Miss Huffberger finished, as proud as if she had invented the pig herself. She turned from the class to Cory. "Thank you for an excellent speech — an 'A' speech, Cory, in spite of rude interruptions." Here she glared again at Andy and Tab. "But I have a question myself. Are your neighbors upset about your keeping a pig?"

Cory shook her head. "No. We haven't told them, though. Why would they care?"

"Because that's the way people are — especially when they're misinformed. Perhaps your neighbors won't be like that.

"All right, class. Who can suggest better ways for us to manage pigs, now that we know the facts?"

The discussion was probably going to be hot, Cory

thought as she scooped up Pandora. She was being excused to go to Robert Lee's classroom in the grade school.

Out on the sidewalk Cory staggered along, with Pandora growing heavier by the second. She felt in her jacket pocket and found the leash. "Great! It's time you walked places," Cory told her as she snapped on the leash.

"Oink," Pandora grunted, planting herself on the sidewalk as she heard the snap of the leash clip.

Cory moved away the full length of the leash. "We're just going one lousy block. Now get up and come on," she ordered with unusual firmness.

Pandora squinted at her and looked unhappy. But slowly she rose to her feet, snout quivering. Snout on the ground, she moved a few inches. "Oink," she grumbled, moving another inch as she inspected the new territory.

It took longer than it was supposed to, but both Cory and Pandora walked to the grade school. Cory had to stop in the girls' bathroom to wash Pandora's snout. She wanted the third grade to see an absolutely pristine piglet.

Robert Lee shot out of his seat as soon as he saw Cory. He took off Pandora's leash and again she pranced around a classroom. Trit, trot, trit, trot. Bouncy, bouncy.

"Lemmee have her!"

"Look at her cute collar!"

"Bug off! It's my turn!"

When Miss Bowen calmed them down, Robert Lee told what he had learned about pigs. Two boys in his class lived on farms, which were fast disappearing as a way of life in New Jersey. They were astounded that Pandora was living in a house as a pet. "Wait'll I tell Dad," one said.

"He won't believe you," said the other.

At the end of his talk Robert Lee sat down, full of success, loving the applause.

Cory and Pandora were escorted to the door by Miss Bowen. She was an older woman who had taught third grade all of her adult life. She whispered into Cory's ear. "Are you saving her manure? It's wonderful for gardens — more natural than all those commercial powders. If you happen to have any extra . . ." She smiled hopefully.

Cory's mind whirled. Here was Miss Bowen positively drooling over pig poop!

"I'll come pick it up," Miss Bowen offered.

Trick and Treat

After Pandora had been to the schools, word spread. Junior-high kids were especially curious.

"Is she still in the house?" one eighth-grader asked.

"Sure," replied Cory. "She's just seven weeks old. She's in a playpen, like any baby."

Eyes bright with fun, Andy stopped by Cory's locker one afternoon just after chorus practice. He leaned toward her and sniffed loudly. "Hmm," he said, "not too fragrant yet."

For a second, Cory was dumbfounded, then she understood. "I told you! Pigs don't stink! Pandora has a bath every day!" She wanted to slug him, but he was too big.

Cory slammed her locker shut and ran down the hall.

"Hey, I was just kidding!" he called after her.

Out on the sidewalk, Willa and Hope were waiting.

"What's the matter?" Hope asked. "You're all red."

"Andy Barton!" was all Cory could say at first. When she calmed down, she told them, ending, "He makes me so mad I could just spit!"

Willa grinned. "He's okay. He doesn't tease *me* any-more — not since I mashed his nose in third grade. But I think he likes you, Cory. He looks at you a lot."

"Yeah," added Hope, "all the time."

Briefly, Cory was flattered. Andy was really cute — if you could forget how he behaved — which she couldn't.

"He makes me sick," she said. "And you guys are crazy. He picks on whoever's handy. It's a good thing summer's coming and I won't see him. Now let's go, okay?"

It was an afternoon in late May, and they were headed for the Deans' house. The three of them nearly always went there when Robert Lee had Scouts or was at a friend's home.

"I brought my shorts," Willa said. "You promised we could go jogging with Pandora."

The Deans now took their pet for a daily jog. Although they stayed in their neighborhood, news of the jogging pig was getting around.

"Is she liking it any better?" Hope asked.

Cory smiled. "You'll see. We only go half a

mile . . . and we're not telling her it's going to get longer. It's Mom's idea. She read us a study about pigs at Arizona State that jog two miles a day."

When the girls opened the back door into the Deans' kitchen, Pandora woke up with a squeal of delight. She spent the hours from eight until four mainly napping, Cory had decided. Pandora would move the toys in her pen a bit and rearrange her towel nest, but there was never a sign that she'd been very active or unhappy during the day.

At four o'clock, things changed. "Wheenk!" she rejoiced, braced on her hind legs, hooves resting on the top metal bar of her pen.

When she was free to run, she made one wild circle around the kitchen. She rubbed against Cory's leg, grunting with pleasure, then took off around the room again.

Cory watched her fondly. So what if kids teased her. They just didn't understand.

"Boy, I wish I had a pig," Willa said.

Hope giggled. "Can you imagine my mom with one?"

Cory laughed with her, but wondered about Gramma. Would Gramma see what a terrific pet Pandora was? I'll make her see, Cory vowed, eager for Gramma's regular visit in June.

The girls changed into shorts and each of them fixed a small treat for Pandora. Cory took the sunglasses on their sports elastic from the counter and put them on.

Pandora wiggled her snout to position the glasses and looked up with a grin. Pigs are not known for smiling, but this pig was definitely doing it. She knew she looked funny and she enjoyed the joke.

"It was Robert Lee's idea," Cory explained as Willa and Hope doubled up. "He thought she was squinting too much on the real sunny days."

Even with her sunglasses, Pandora didn't care for exercise. She made it clear, oinking in a disapproving manner, that she was jogging under protest — and only for the expected, tasty bribes.

"Better give her the peanut butter sandwich now," Cory told Willa after a few blocks.

On with the jog. "That's a good girl," Cory said, keeping a steady pull on the leash. "What a good, big, healthy girl we're going to be."

Pandora sat down and Cory turned to Hope. "It's time for those potato chips."

A few noisy crunches and the chips were gone. Above all things, Pandora loved junk food. And it was Robert Lee's fault. Whenever she did a trick for him — or did only what she was supposed to — he gave her a treat. Pizza, bits of chocolate, chips and pretzels, cookies and cake. She adored them all. Her favorite was Coca-Cola, which she guzzled out of the bottle.

Cory had warned him. "If Mom catches you giving her that stuff, she's going to explode. And you know it!"

Robert Lee was unconvinced. "Mom said pigs are

happy eating just what people eat. I eat this stuff and
I'm fine!" Since Robert Lee was the healthiest child
in third grade, he had a point, and the argument usually died there.

Now, Pandora's snout had located the last morsel of
potato chip and she consented to jog again. Cory added
one extra block to their route, keeping a steady pull
on the leash until they got back home.

Once inside the gate, Pandora sat down and opened
her mouth. She grunted, waiting.

Cory gave her the pear she'd been saving.

"Wrunk, wrunk." Fruit was the next best thing to a
bottle of Coke.

Hope brought the hose around to the front sidewalk
for Pandora's shower, a real necessity for the hot little
pig. She had a plastic wading pool of clean water in
her new outdoor pen, but she liked a shower better.
When Cory shut her in the pen, she began to root
contentedly through the grass and weedy patches.

Indoors, with popcorn and Cokes, Cory and her
friends wished for summer. "It better hurry up and get
here," Willa said through a mouthful of popcorn.
"Math, language arts, science — borr-rring. I can't
wait for camp!"

Cory and Hope looked at each other. Hope asked,
"You're still staying? You're not going to Kentucky with
Robert Lee, are you?"

"I'm staying, but wait'll you hear what Mom thinks
I should do — besides diving lessons, I mean." She

explained her mother's plan for their manure pile and how it was supposed to earn money.

"And Robert Lee's teacher, old Miss Bowen? She already asked if she could have some! Can you believe that?"

"Let her have all she wants. Then you won't have to sell any," Willa said.

"Ha!" Cory stopped lounging in her chair and sat up. "We read that a one-hundred-ten-pound pig makes a ton of poop a year. A ton! *Two thousand pounds.*"

"That's too much for Miss Bowen," Hope observed.

"No lie!" Cory said, laughing with Willa.

Hope was not laughing. Her fair, pleasant face was wrinkled in thought. You could almost see her brain cells scurrying around.

"Well?" prompted Cory after a long silence.

"I think . . ." Hope frowned harder.

"You do? We weren't ever sure," Willa said.

Hope made a face at her. "I think," she began again, "that you can make more money with pig poop than I can being a mother's helper."

"It's totally gross stuff!" moaned Cory. "How would you like to haul pig poop all over town?"

"Look, Cory," Hope went on, "I've helped in our garden for years, and fertilizer costs a fortune. We're always looking for good stuff from farms, you know —"

"*The real thing,*" Cory said, sighing. "I can't believe it. That's just what Mom said — all gardeners want manure."

Hope nodded solemnly. "You could put it in grocery bags. Who'd know? People who want lots of it would come in their cars. You'd have your very own business."

Mrs. Dean came into the kitchen then, dropping her load of books and papers on the stool by the door. "Phew! It's hot for May. You girls gave Pandora a shower after her run, I trust?" She paused, eyeing them. "Why so glum? Is something the matter?"

"Summer," Cory said.

"Aah." Her mother poured a glass of juice and joined them at the table. "You don't want to sell manure, lots of kids will be gone, and you will be bored, right?"

Cory just nodded.

Willa said, "I'll be at camp."

And Hope said, "I think your manure idea's great, Mrs. Dean. My folks'll buy some for sure."

"You sell it then," Cory told her.

"I can help! The places I baby-sit are just stuffed with flowers . . . vegetables . . . raspberries . . ." — her hands were measuring miles of gardens — "and everybody wants —"

"*The real thing!*" chimed Cory and Willa.

When the laughter subsided, Mrs. Dean leaned forward. "Listen, troops, I had an idea about summer. I had lunch with Professor James again today — of course, he's keeping tabs on Pandora, since she's one of his pigs — and his daughter is teaching crafts in a local park. And I said to myself, wow! What about an old-fashioned summer?"

Here we go again, Cory thought.

"Don't look so skeptical. Remember, long ago, when girls made quilts and knitted socks? Argyle socks are very popular now. And maybe just a quilted pillow at first, to see if you like it? Gramma could get you started when she comes, but I love knitting and quilting and I have nearly two months free this summer. What do you think?"

Hmmm, mused Cory. I spent half an hour just putting on a button once. Hope will probably like sewing though, so maybe . . . She tried to imagine her summer. Diving, argyle socks, and manure. It would be different anyway — unlike anyone else's summer. She had always loved argyle socks and sweaters.

"Well," she began, wishing she could think about it longer. Sewing? When it was hot?

"I'm making a whole quilt, not just a pillow," Hope announced. "I don't care if it takes till I'm married."

Willa leaned forward. "I don't go to camp till the first of July. I'll do quilted pillows for my bed."

"You'll have at least one finished before you leave for camp," Mrs. Dean promised. "You can take the pieces for another one with you."

Somehow, by the time Hope and Willa left, Cory's summer was all laid out. Hope had vowed to promote the manure business wherever she went, and maybe she would be right about all the money Cory could make. And, compared to sewing or knitting, having her own business would be fun. Now if I could only forget it's manure, she thought.

· After dinner that evening, when Pandora had had a short nap, Mrs. Dean called out, "Okay, time for school."

Cory and Robert Lee took turns helping their mother to train Pandora. Mrs. Dean insisted on this. The piglet must obey all of them, not just one person. Tonight was Cory's turn to help.

Pandora knew it was time for lessons. She parked herself by Mrs. Dean, who was seated at the kitchen table, and opened her mouth. When nothing happened, she bumped Mrs. Dean's leg and opened her mouth wider.

In went a tiny square of peanut butter sandwich.

Pandora smiled up at Cory's mother.

"What a good girl!" Mrs. Dean said as she rubbed behind the piglet's ears. "Come on, into the bathroom. Here we go. Stand up tall. Hooves on the rim. Push hard with your snout. Ooh, look at the lovely water."

"Whink!" agreed Pandora.

She was learning to flush the toilet. Her need for fresh water was great. Soon she'd be bigger, out of her playpen, and in need of much more water than a pet bowl could supply. It had been Cory's idea to teach her to drink from the toilet, just as their cats did.

Now Mrs. Dean braced Pandora's front hooves on the rim of the low bowl. "Nice water," she said, pushing Pandora's snout down.

Cory went through the routine the next time. When Pandora made the toilet flush or took a drink, she got another bite of sandwich.

Because the piglet was so young, her training sessions lasted only fifteen minutes. When the time was nearly up, Pandora searched the kitchen floor for any stray crumbs, then trotted into the bathroom. She stood up, flushed the toilet with her snout, and watched while the bowl filled. She looked back over her shoulder at Cory and Mrs. Dean standing in the doorway.

"Wheeeenk!" she squealed before bending down to drink.

That was worth a whole pear.

Andy should see this, Cory thought. He thinks he's *so smart*. Hah!

"Brightest animal I've ever trained," Mrs. Dean said as she wrote in Pandora's learning record.

"If she could reach the kitchen faucets . . . ," Cory began.

"Oh, don't even think it!"

"Right," Cory agreed. "It's dumb." But she was remembering something else she had thought was dumb at the time — a remark that just wouldn't go away.

"Mom, have any neighbors complained about Pandora?"

Her mother stopped writing and looked up. "No. Why? Has someone spoken to you?"

"No, but Miss Huffberger thinks they will. She said city people wouldn't understand, and so they'd complain."

Mrs. Dean leaned back, tapping her pen on the table. "She could be right. Professor James said something similar. But she's so small . . . and our yard's enormous. Her pen isn't close to anyone else's property."

"The manure pile is. It's pretty close to the Finnegans' yard, don't you think?"

"Our lovely compost heap? It's behind their garage — and two hundred feet from their house if it's an inch!"

"Yes, but they don't know us at all. Could they make trouble?"

"I suppose, but I'll handle it." She stood up abruptly. "I'll check into the zoning laws about animals. And don't you worry, okay?"

Cory nodded, only partly reassured.

The Ham
What Am

Summer followed rapidly after the warm days of May. By mid-June school was out. Yea, no more Andy! Cory rejoiced. And I'm a seventh-grader.

But those weren't the only changes. Pandora had become a teenager.

Mom was right, Cory thought, nudging their porker off the scale. She had been a baby a terribly short time. Now the scale read fifty pounds when four hooves stepped on it.

Pandora loved being a teenager. Where her playpen had once stood, there was only the litter pan and her towel nest. She had the run of the house . . . and she knew how to run it.

Whenever Cory read on the couch, Pandora kept up a steady lament until she was on the couch too, her head in Cory's lap.

Rain and Drizzle would sleep nearby in a chair, now and then opening one eye to glare at the intruder. Because of her, their food was now on top of the refrigerator where Pandora couldn't reach it. If they chose to have a sip of water in the bathroom, along would come Pandora, who always flushed the toilet in their faces.

Pandora met all guests at the front door. She peered at them through the window beside the door and called "Weee!" until one of the Deans came running. Each guest underwent a thorough inspection, toe to knee.

Pandora's learning record was crammed with accomplishments. Thanks to loving care, a nearly perfect diet, and regular exercise, she had become the ultimate piglet. Her personality blossomed.

· The first Saturday morning after school was out, Mrs. Dean said, "Okay, who's been eating all the fruit? I filled the crisper yesterday — for the third time this week — and it's empty again."

"Not me, boy!" answered Robert Lee.

Cory said, "I gave Pandora a pear after jogging last night, and I had an apple. That's all."

Her mom went back to the grocery store, treated everyone to doughnuts, and refilled the crisper with fruit.

That evening, she began preparing dinner early because they were going to Newark Airport to meet Gramma, who was coming for her summer visit.

Cory was happily throwing out her old school note-books when she heard her mother calling.

"Everybody come to the kitchen. Right away!"

When Cory, Robert Lee, and Pandora arrived in the kitchen, they saw an empty crisper on the table. "This has gone far enough," Mrs. Dean announced. "Now, who ate it?"

Cory and Robert Lee looked at one another and shook their heads. Then they looked at Pandora.

Pandora edged over toward her nest of towels. She snouted them into position and lay down, head stretched out on the floor. She closed her eyes.

Mrs. Dean looked from the kids to Pandora and back again. "Oh, come on! You're not suggesting —"

"You bet!" Cory said. "We couldn't eat all that fruit. We'd be sick. Right, Robert Lee?"

"Right!"

"I'd like to see just how she manages to get the refrigerator door open. *And* get into the crisper," their mother replied.

"Let's put more fruit in it and go outside and spy on her through a window," Robert Lee suggested.

"It's her snout," said Cory. "She can do almost anything with it."

"Well, it's a very sneaky snout," Mrs. Dean said, banging the dinner plates down on the table. "And I'm putting the fruit up higher from now on.

"Robert Lee, give her only half of a regular dinner. She's had more than enough today!"

Before they left for the airport, Mrs. Dean borrowed one pear from a neighbor. She put it in the crisper, in the normal place. "If it's gone when we return," she said, "then we'll know for sure."

Cory and her brother exchanged glances again. They already knew for sure. When the car motor came to life, Cory listened out the window. "WEEE!" she heard, carrying clearly from the house to the driveway. Pandora was missing a car ride and she knew it. Her cry followed them out the drive.

· When Gramma met them in the airport she hugged everyone, told Cory and Robert Lee how tall they'd gotten, and asked, "Where's the pig? Holding the fort at home alone?"

"Possibly eating a pear at home alone," Mrs. Dean replied. "We think she's figured out how to raid the refrigerator."

"How clever," Gramma said. "I can hardly wait to meet her. I hope you told her I'm not standing for any nonsense from a pig."

At that Mrs. Dean smiled. "Oh, we told her, but I'm not sure she believes us. Really, Mother, she's been an absolute delight. You'll see."

"Mom's right this time," Cory added, squeezing Gramma's hand. "Honest. She's the best pet we ever had."

On the hour-long drive home, Cory and Robert Lee told Gramma what they'd been doing since she last visited them over Easter. Gramma showed Cory the beautiful yarns she had brought for the matching argyle socks and sweater.

"I brought some for myself," she said. "I think argyle socks will look pretty spiffy on the racquetball court." Gramma played racquetball every morning before going off to manage a huge staff of hospital volunteers. She slept only six hours a night, drank a vodka gimlet cocktail before dinner, and wore red pantsuits. The hospital patients and staff loved her as much as Cory and Robert Lee did.

At home, as soon as they were in the kitchen, Mrs. Dean opened the refrigerator and checked its crisper.

"It's gone! Vanished!"

Pandora stopped inspecting Gramma and trotted over to the refrigerator. She poked her snout into the crisper, then looked up at Mrs. Dean. "Wee?" she asked hopefully.

Gramma began to chuckle. "I may enjoy this after all," she said. "This is the cleanest pig I've ever seen."

"And the smartest!" Robert Lee said proudly, rubbing the piglet's back. "Gramma, can we play poker now?"

Cory, Gramma, and Robert Lee loved the marathon poker game that would last all month. Each player began with a hundred poker chips. Anyone who ran out of chips had to sing a song, recite a poem, or do a dance — whatever the others decided — before a hundred more chips were issued.

While Cory was counting out the chips, Mrs. Dean got out Pandora's learning record. "I just know Professor James is going to find this latest trick terribly amusing," she said. She did not sound amused herself.

"I missed my gimlet," Gramma announced, rummaging in the back of the games cupboard. Mrs. Dean drank only wine, and not often, but she kept vodka for her mother's cocktails.

"It's in there somewhere, Mother, just keep hunting," Mrs. Dean said vaguely, concerned with her pig record.

At last they were settled on the living room floor, ready for a game of twenty-one. Gramma sipped her drink, set it beside her, and spread out the cards. "Draw for the deal," she said. "I'll play an hour, kids. Then I want to visit with your mother, and we'll play more tomorr —"

A noisy slurp interrupted. Another slurp.

"Pandora!" yelled Cory.

"WEE!" Pandora scolded, reminding Cory not to yell.

Gramma snatched up her glass. "Dang her! She got most of it. Left me only the ice cubes."

"Cocktails aren't good for you anyway," Mrs. Dean said, trying not to laugh.

"Says who? At my age I can do what I please. No pig is going to run *my* life. You can bet your bippy on that!"

Gramma stood up. "We play at the table from now

on. And you," she told Pandora, "had better keep your snout to yourself. Hear me?"

Pandora smiled up at her.

"She's laughing at me!" said Gramma.

Mrs. Dean looked up from her writing. "Yes, she has quite a sense of humor. I really am sorry about your drink, Mother, but pigs love alcohol. Like humans, I'm afraid. A pig will happily drink itself into a stupor."

"Not while I'm around it won't!" Gramma got the vodka bottle out of the low cupboard and marched toward the kitchen. "I'm hiding it where she'll never find it."

Cory and Robert Lee began gathering up chips and cards to move the poker game to the kitchen table.

"Good God Almighty!" came Gramma's voice. "Somebody get in here! There's the most appalling odor —"

"Uh oh, Pandora's done it again," Robert Lee whispered to Cory. "Take it out, quick."

"You take it. It's your turn."

"It is not! I did it this afternoon!"

"Well I did it after dinner!" Cory retorted.

Their mother said, "Oh hush. I'll get it this time. Bring the poker stuff and quit arguing."

In the kitchen Gramma had pushed up a screen and was leaning out the window, breathing deeply of the night air.

Mrs. Dean whisked the litter pan outdoors and returned to spray the room with a fresh pine scent. Gramma's upper half was still outside, her bottom inside.

"You can come in now, Mother," Mrs. Dean said. "I sprayed and it smells fine."

Gramma March backed out of the window, stood upright, and faced her daughter. "Amanda," she began ominously.

Mrs. Dean held up one hand. "Before you get all excited, let me explain that we rarely have this problem. The kids take turns removing the manure and we do it immediately so there's no odor. Sometimes we have to spray with a room deodorizer, but not often."

"Pig manure is the most revolting smell —"

Cory agreed, but she had to defend Pandora. "Honest, Gramma, we hardly ever have a stink like this." She rushed on, unthinking, "And I'm going to make tons of money this summer from our compost heap. So it's worth it, see?"

Gramma looked at Cory and slowly went from boil to simmer. After a time she said, "You mean you're *saving* all of it? Where, for heaven's sake?"

"Out back. Way out back. It's a real compost heap. Mom studied how to do it," explained Cory. "Gramma, people with gardens are just dying for the real thing." And Cory found herself believing it. Even Hope had known.

A faint smile touched Gramma's face. "The real thing, huh? Well your stuff is as real as it ever gets! And I won't have anything to do with it. When I holler for someone to come take it out, you'd better show up on the double." She turned to Robert Lee. "You, too, buddy."

"Yes, Gramma," he said. "Can we play poker now?"

Gramma sat down and began shuffling the cards. "I'm surprised your neighbors haven't had a fit," she said.

"There's almost no odor from the compost," Mrs. Dean replied. "Nobody even knows or cares about one measly pig."

"I find that very hard to believe," said Gramma, passing the deck to Robert Lee. "It's still your deal. Be good to me this time."

Pandora's Products, Inc.

After her defense of Pandora — or rather, the smell she had made — Cory knew she was committed. No going back now, no changing her mind. She was president of Pig Poop, Incorporated and that was that. Hadn't she told Gramma so herself?

By bedtime that night, Cory had definite ideas for her business. Might as well go whole hog, she thought, giggling. Tomorrow I'll call Hope, so she can start selling. But we're going to call it something else. Not fertilizer or manure or poop.

Maybe Cory's Compost? Yuk! I don't want my name on it! Or Deans' Delicate Mixture? Ha-ha. How about Grow-More for Gardens? That was boring. It was so boring she fell asleep.

Sunday morning, as she was getting ready for

church, Cory thought of the perfect name: Pandora's Products, Inc. She would draw a pig portrait on each sack of compost.

"You certainly sang hymns with a will today," Gramma told Cory as they drove home after church. Gramma belted out each hymn as if it were her school's fight song.

"Thanks, Gramma." She couldn't explain that her newfound enthusiasm for selling pig manure had made her feel good in church. No. Some things could not be explained.

At home, Gramma began fixing lunch while Pandora went for her Sunday drive with Mrs. Dean and Robert Lee.

"Yes, Mother, I know it's ridiculous," Mrs. Dean said, "but Pandora loves riding in the car. I'd do the same for *you* if you enjoyed it as much as she does."

Cory called Hope. "And so each bag will have Pandora's picture on it. What do you think?"

"It's a real personal touch," Hope said. "I like the word *products*, too. It makes it better, somehow."

Even though Hope couldn't see her, Cory nodded happily. Hope was very good about understanding things. That's why she was such a satisfactory friend.

"I'll get started right now," Hope promised. "I can call at least ten places today before I go baby-sitting. This's going to make a fortune, Cory, you just wait."

Cory set the table for Gramma and went out to check

their compost heap. Headquarters for Pandora's Products, Inc., was at the very back of their lot, under the eaves of an old shed. Mrs. Dean claimed that hammering and pounding projects were psychologically healthy, and she had built the long compost bin.

By now, the chopped-straw bedding and manure were nearly two feet deep. They had turned the mixture frequently and kept it from drying out with a plastic cover. It was the loveliest compost heap in New Jersey.

I can work out of the shed, Cory decided, pushing open its nearly rotten door. She imagined the neat stacks of grocery bags, her pink crayon for drawing, and the list of orders — all tidily arranged. And now she needed that list.

After lunch, Pandora went outdoors for her daily rooting session. Cory filled the pig's wading pool and set out to find her customers.

"Fresh stuff? Real manure?" Mr. Branley said, eyes glowing. "Here I've seen you running with that pig and never even thought!" He paused, figuring. "About four bags, I'd guess. How soon can I have it?"

Hand shaking with excitement, Cory wrote down the order. Four bags! At two dollars a bag, she had just earned eight dollars in about one minute. She promised Mr. Branley delivery later that day and went to the next house.

The next house was the same, only Mrs. Dietrich ordered five bags. Her neighbor ordered three. And so it went, for over an hour. Mom and Hope were right, she exulted. City people are just dying for the real thing!

By the time Cory returned home, she had orders for twenty-eight bags of compost. Overnight she had become president of a fantastic, incredible business. But . . . all of the customers were counting on home delivery. Right away.

Shovel in hand, Cory marched to the compost heap. She moved all of the "good" stuff, that which had lost its pungent odor, to one end of the bin. It could be delivered now. The really fresh manure and bedding she shifted to the opposite end. It's got to wait and decompose more, she thought, nose wrinkled in disgust.

That done, she went inside the shed to draw Pandora's picture on the bags. With Cory's business in mind, Mrs. Dean had been saving grocery bags for weeks. She had told people in her office and they had donated many.

Now, Cory hummed and drew pig portraits until twenty-eight bags were decorated. Then she began shoveling manure into them. Filling the bags was hard, smelly, sweaty work. At the end, she couldn't wait to jump into the shower.

And finally, wearing clean shorts and a T-shirt, she loaded ten bags into the red wagon and began delivering.

"Wonderful, wonderful," exulted Mr. Branley as he lifted his four bags out of her wagon.

All of her customers were excited. Mrs. Dietrich said, "Just bring me the same amount next month, all right?"

Cory was standing beside her last wagonload of Pandora's Products, checking her order list, when a bike screeched to a stop at the curb beside her.

"Hey! Whatcha doing?"

Oh no! Of all kids! Without looking up from her list, she knew exactly who it was.

"What's on those bags?" Andy got off his bike and bent down to examine the pink picture on each sack.

Cory felt her temper and her face flare at the same moment. "What are you doing in my neighborhood anyway?"

He looked up, grinning. "That's not very friendly."

"I don't feel friendly."

"Yeah, I can tell," he said, grin fading. He patted a sack. "That's a great-looking pig. Did you draw it?"

"Yes." Oh, if he would *only* go away. But he wouldn't, not till he knew the truth. Not Andy. He couldn't fool her with that smile, either. She had known him too long.

And she was tired of being the object of his jokes. It's time I fought back, she decided, remembering what Willa had said about mashing his nose. From deep inside, Cory gathered up her courage and her pride. This was a real business and that was what counted.

"That's pig manure," she announced loudly. "Great

stuff, pig manure. I'm making so much money you wouldn't believe it."

"No lie? People pay real money for —"

"You bet!" she interrupted before he had a chance to make fun of her and her business. "Two dollars a bag, and they want me to deliver more every month. It's the best business I've ever been in," she added, chin high, as if she ran a different business every summer.

"Hey . . . that's terrific," Andy said. He smiled openly at her — warmly even.

Like her brother, he had an irresistible smile. Cory found herself smiling back. At Andy Barton of all people! I must be crazy, she thought. "Well," she said briskly, "I have to make some more deliveries. Bye."

Andy pedaled his bike next to the curb, only two feet away from her. "Aren't those bags kind of heavy?" he asked.

"No."

"They look heavy."

"Well, they're not."

Creak, creak went the wagon wheels. Cory darted a sideways glance at Andy, and he was frowning, deep in thought.

After a bit he said, "I don't have anything to do."

"I can tell."

"Look, I'm trying to be nice!"

"Why?" Cory glanced at him again, then stared

straight ahead before he caught her. It was just lovely having Andy Barton suffer. It was his turn.

Andy sighed noisily. "You're sure making this hard."

"Making what hard?" Cory said, beginning to enjoy herself. At last she had figured out how to handle Andy Barton. Only took me six years, she thought wryly.

Cory checked house numbers, stopped the wagon, and bent down to pick up a loaded bag.

"I'll get it!" he yelled, dropping his bike.

Andy carried all four bags around to the Shafers' back garden. Cory let him.

"Same order next month, Mr. Shafer?" Andy asked before Cory had a chance.

"Guess so. Good thought, son," Mr. Shafer said, smiling at both Andy and Cory.

Back on the sidewalk with the wagon, Cory said, "Look here, this's *my business*. I don't need you."

"But, see . . . I can do the heavy stuff, like filling the bags and carrying them. It's going to be a real hot summer. You won't like all the heavy stuff."

I don't believe this, Cory thought. "How do you know it's going to be hot?" she asked weakly.

"Because the woolly bears have real thin coats. Trust Mother Nature," he said, grinning.

Cory returned the grin uncertainly, her head spinning. At last she said, "But you live far away."

"Yeah, and nothing's happening in my neighborhood. I mean, nothing! But this is fun. I like it."

He *likes* it, she thought. Oh whoopee. Who'd have believed this? Out loud she said, "Look, I need the money from this job, so I can't —"

"Did I say you had to pay me?"

"No . . . but it isn't fair —"

"Okay, okay! So, if you want . . . after a while . . . if I help a lot, I mean . . . and you think it's worth it . . . then you can give me a little bit. How's that?" Again the smile.

Cory looked at the ground. *Now* what should she say? He really was trying to be nice. Were Hope and Willa right? Did Andy Barton like her . . . *a lot?*

She remembered filling the bags with compost. It had been horrible work — grubby and slow. But here stood Andy, offering to help.

"I guess we could try it once," she said finally. "But *I* take the orders. It's *my business*."

"Great! Let's go get some more bags."

"That's it for today. Twenty-eight bags. I've got fifty-six dollars in my pocket."

"Hey, that's cool! What're you going to do with it?"

"I don't know for sure." Cory began pulling the wagon back toward home. "Save it, I guess. Maybe buy a real TV. We've got this teeny black-and-white antique."

Andy made a face. "That's *all?*"

"Yeah. Mom says kids shouldn't watch TV all the time."

"Oh, one of those kind of mothers," he said.

She nodded. "Whenever Mom has any extra money she buys books. We look like the public library."

In no time, or so it seemed, they were at Cory's house.

"When should I come back?" Andy asked.

"A couple days, I guess." And maybe that would be too soon. Cory was afraid she couldn't trust him to be nice.

"Right!" he said. "See you Tuesday!" He zoomed down the driveway and pedaled away, leaving her to wonder why he had changed so much.

If I can get up the guts, she thought, I'm going to come right out and ask him sometime!

· The next day, on Monday, Gramma began the sewing projects, because Mrs. Dean was working until early July.

"All the pieces must be cut exactly to size," she explained to Willa and Hope, her quilters.

Cory struggled with knit two, purl two as she began the ribbing on her first pair of argyle socks. "Gramma," she said after a few rows, "Every time I do a row, I have a different number of stitches!"

"Here, let me see," Gramma said. "Well, honey, I think you just need to be a bit more patient. Remember, the design starts after only three inches. Then it's really fun. How about another glass of lemonade, girls?"

Afternoons, Cory took orders for Pandora's Products or delivered them, going farther and farther from her house as the days went by. On delivery days, Andy came, right on time and smiling.

Cory couldn't make herself ask him why he had changed, why he was being so friendly. She couldn't completely relax with him yet, either. It was weird.

Still, she sold sixty bags that first week, and forty-five the second week, earning $210.00. Andy had loaded and lugged nearly all of those bags. She made him take twenty dollars, and gave Robert Lee ten for carting poop out to the compost heap.

When Robert Lee left for Kentucky, he took five dollars with him and gave Pandora a whole candy bar in farewell.

Of the $180.00 left, Cory kept out thirty — for movies, maybe, or new tapes for the Walkman Gramma had given her last Christmas. The rest she banked, saving for a new TV.

· The first Monday in July found Mrs. Dean, Cory, and Pandora in the car, on their way to the vet for a checkup.

"I'd rather be dead than doing this," Cory moaned.

Pandora poked her head out the window, snout quivering in appreciation. Every now and then she went "Whink!" so that her family would know how much she was enjoying herself.

As soon as they got out of the car, Pandora took one

look at the clinic and plopped her bottom on the ground. "Oink," she grunted, snout thrust forward belligerently.

"She remembers," Cory said. "I knew she would. Now what're we going to do?"

At sixty pounds, all in a low, compact mass, Pandora was far too heavy for either of them to lift. Mrs. Dean went inside the vet's clinic and came back out with the kennel boy, Michael. Michael carried a stout wooden crate with a removable floor. Before Pandora knew what was happening, he set the crate down on top of her and slid the floor into place underneath her hooves.

"EEEE!" screamed Pandora as she realized she'd been tricked. "EEEEEE!"

The Deans' pig hollered all the way into the vet's office. When Michael set her crate down on the examining table, she tried to bite him through the wooden slats.

He jumped aside, grinning. "Ha-ha, piggy. Gotcha this time." To Mrs. Dean he said, "Next time, she'll be on the lookout for that crate. You should think of another way before then, okay? See ya around." He left the room.

Pandora stopped shrieking and glared at Cory and Mrs. Dean. She bumped her snout against the slats, trying to force her way out.

Dr. Sam slipped in the door, looked at each of

them in turn, and understood the situation. "Right!" he said briefly. "I'll handle this. You two ladies pop on out to the waiting room and reassure everyone that I'm not butchering a pig back here. When I'm finished, I'll put her in your car and we can talk. Go on, now."

They didn't need persuading. Out in the waiting room, Mrs. Dean said, "Excuse me, but our pig is back there for a routine checkup, and it's possible that we might hear —"

"EEEEE! EEEEEEEE! EEEEEEEEEE!"

Cory covered her ears. Only an angry pig, she knew now, could make these piercing, agonized cries. Pandora was telling the world that she was being tortured, flayed alive, turned into bacon, strip by strip. And none of it was true, of course. Dr. Sam was the kindest of men. The worst that could possibly happen was a shot, maybe two.

"EEEEE! EEEEEEE!"

The people in the waiting room shifted uneasily, eyes wide as they listened. The dogs crept behind their owners' legs. The cats hunkered down, quivering, ears laid back.

Mrs. Dean was furious. "That's just temper," she announced. "It's her worst fault, and I can't seem to do anything about it."

At last, a heavenly peace settled on the clinic. Dr. Sam entered the waiting room, carrying the crated pig and singing, "Oh what a beautiful pig-let, Oh what a glorious pig. . . ." He winked at Cory and her mother.

Pandora glared balefully out through the slats.

"Meet you back in my office," Dr. Sam said, going out the door to the parking lot.

Seconds later, seated behind his desk, Dr. Sam assured them that Pandora was a perfect specimen. "Not so much soap," he suggested. "She's getting dandruff. Her weight gain is good, about three quarters of a pound a day. I'd guess she'll weigh around a hundred thirty pounds at six months, and she'll continue to add a bit till she's a year old."

He looked up from Pandora's record. "No problems at all that I can see. Except . . . has a fellow named Finnegan said anything to you about keeping her in town? He's a neighbor of yours, I believe."

"He hasn't spoken to me," replied Mrs. Dean. "I've rarely seen him, but his lot is directly behind ours."

"He bought four bags of compost," Cory said, "and he was all excited about it."

"Well, he was in here last week with his Saint Bernard," Dr. Sam went on. "Seems he's not real happy about a pig living near his house. I got the feeling he might be talking to other people, too."

I just knew it, Cory thought miserably. Miss Huffberger was right. People don't understand.

"I don't care for people who talk behind my back!" snapped Mrs. Dean. "Why doesn't he tell *me?*"

"I couldn't agree with you more," said the vet. "But I thought you ought to know." He rose. "Anyway, you're doing a beautiful job, and next time I'll check Miss Pandora at your place. That will be easier for everyone."

Swimming Weather

With the coming of July, summer settled down on
Rocky Brook like a heavy, smothering blanket. Andy
and the woolly bears had been right. Cory couldn't
remember a summer this hot. She and Hope began
diving lessons and Willa left for camp. Gramma fixed
cold salads for dinners while Rain and Drizzle dozed
near the front door, waiting for a puff of cooler air.
Pandora stayed in the shade, in her pool.

In the early evenings, Gramma and Mrs. Dean went
to the pool for adult swimming. Pandora had her
nightly shower.

"EEEE!" she scolded when Cory turned off the
water.

"*She talks,*" Andy said, shaking his head with wonder. He had come to personally witness a pig in the

shower. He insisted on patting water off Pandora's back so she wouldn't drip all over the house.

Head partly hidden by the giant towel, Andy said, "I'm sorry I gave you such a bad time. She's a really cool pet."

He was apologizing. Andy Barton, himself. Was he growing up? Was that what seventh grade did to people?

Andy kept on toweling Pandora and didn't look up.

"It's okay," she said, feeling shy and awkward. Odd how she didn't want him to suffer anymore. But then, he'd worked hard at her business, never wanting any money, though she always shared.

He looked at her then. "I could come to the pool tomorrow, after diving lessons."

Cory's remaining doubts flew away. He did like her. A lot. She wished she had put on clean clothes before he came. Or combed her hair.

Finding her voice at last, she said, "That'd be fun."

· Cory spent more and more time at the pool as the heat intensified. She didn't work very hard at selling Pandora's Products. Having liberally supplied the neighborhood, she had to seek customers many blocks away. Anyhow, she thought, who can grub around in gardens when it's this icky?

When they talked to Robert Lee on Sundays, Cory

told him, "We're just swimming and sewing. Some of Hope's baby-sitting families have come for manure, but it's too hot for hauling it around. You're not missing a thing, honest."

As the sweltering days dragged on, Mrs. Dean told Cory that it was too steamy for her traditional birthday picnic. "I've got a terrific idea instead," she said. "Ask Hope to come on Saturday, all dressed up, and we four ladies will do something special."

The something special was lunch in an elegant French inn on the Delaware River, just across the line into Pennsylvania. They ate coq au vin — delicious chicken in wine sauce with mushrooms and vegetables — carrot soufflé, and for dessert, chocolate mousse cake. Everyone in the restaurant sang "Happy Birthday" as their waiter approached with the candle-lit cake.

"I am moving to France," Cory announced, licking the last bits from her cake fork.

"I'll settle for a live-in French cook," said Gramma.

Hope said, "Mrs. Dean, this was the nicest birthday party I've ever —"

"But we're not finished," interrupted Cory's mother. "In fact, we should hurry up. I have tickets for *South Pacific* at the Bucks County Playhouse. The lovely air-conditioned playhouse," she added with a smile.

Without thinking Cory said, "Isn't this getting kind of expensive?" Then she was embarrassed. Only a class-A nerd would bring up the cost of a party in front of guests.

Her mother continued to smile anyway. "We deserve it," she said, leaning forward confidentially. "This is really a party for *two of us*. I'm supposed to be quiet until a formal announcement next week, but I've gotten a raise and a promotion. I'm now head of student psychological services as well as my department, and I'm very excited about it."

Gramma clapped her hands with pleasure. Everyone congratulated Mrs. Dean all the way to the car.

"I should never have mentioned it," Mrs. Dean said. "This is supposed to be Cory's day, remember?"

As she got into bed that night, Cory felt more than content with her day. The music from *South Pacific* was still singing in her head. Gramma had given both girls a tape of the musical as a souvenir of the day. Cory had new clothes, a silver necklace that Willa had wrapped and left before she went to camp, and a musical jewelry box from Hope. Andy had given her a rose red T-shirt that matched Pandora's leash.

And Mom has a wonderful new job, she thought, yawning happily into her pillow. Professor James is even taking her out to celebrate. Cory remembered the times her mother had mentioned having lunch with the agronomy professor. He was "keeping tabs on Pandora," she always said.

Oh yeah? she thought, full of new knowledge. If a

guy keeps making excuses to see somebody . . . I'll bet there's more to this than a pig. But he has a daughter. How can he take Mom out if he's married?

· Professor James rang their doorbell as the hall clock chimed seven on the following Friday evening.

"Weee!" called their self-appointed official greeter.

When Cory got to the door, she saw a big man kneeling outside the screen and making faces at Pandora.

"Rats," he said, standing up as quickly as his long legs would allow. "Now my dignity's shot all to hell. I never learn. Hi, there. You must be Cory."

He attempted to smooth a mass of graying, dark hair — a hopeless gesture. Cory could tell at once that his hair had never behaved itself. He was smiling down at her now and she smiled back. Anybody would, she thought. He was awfully good looking even if he was old. His large, craggy face reminded her of somebody carved on Mount Rushmore.

"Do you suppose I could come in?"

"Oh, sorry. Pandora, get out of the way!"

Professor James, once inside, went back down on his knees and began feeling Pandora all over. "Ooh, she's a beauty, isn't she?" he said to Cory.

"Wrunk," murmured Pandora, her snout busily exploring Professor James's right ear.

"You won't find anything good in there," he told her. "I washed it just last spring."

Cory giggled. "Mom's coming right down. Gramma's helping her because she can't reach all the buttons on the back of her dress. It's new."

When Mrs. Dean entered the living room, Professor James forgot Pandora. He rose to his feet, never taking his eyes off Cory's mother.

"Wow," he breathed.

Wow is right, thought Cory. The only other time she had seen a man look at a woman like that was in the movies.

Mrs. Dean introduced Gramma, who had been eyeing the professor from the doorway. "Mother's come all the way from Washington, D.C., to be my professional dresser," she said, laughing. "It seems I've bought a garment I cannot put on without help."

"And you can't wear it to the office either," Professor James said. "It's much too . . . too fetching." He made another swipe at his mop of hair.

Her mother turned pink and Cory thought, *yup*. This is a *lot* more than shared interest in a pig.

After she and Gramma had waved them good-bye, Gramma put on their *South Pacific* tape. They played it quite loud, something Cory's mom never appreciated. "It's better this way," Gramma said. "We can close our eyes and imagine we're in the theater again."

During a quieter part, when Bloody Mary was singing "Bali Hai," Cory said, "He's in love with her, isn't he?"

"Head over heels," Gramma replied, knowing that

Cory meant Professor James. She moved closer on the couch so they could talk without having to shout over the music.

"I liked him though," Gramma went on. "Liked him right away. He seems to be a good person. He'd have to be or she wouldn't be seeing him. She had the best in your dad, remember? She won't settle for less, don't you worry."

"But he's got a daughter!"

"Yes, and a son, and both are in college," Gramma said. "Your mother told me when I was helping her dress. His wife died some time ago, so I expect he's lonesome. And your mother is a very pretty woman. Nice, too," added Gramma.

"I know. But, Gramma, we didn't think there was anybody special. Mom mostly talks about the ladies she works with, not the men. When she talked about Professor James, it was always something to do with Pandora."

Cory frowned. That was how she thought of him — as Pandora's father. But if he was in love with her mother, then he might become *hers* too.

"We don't need a father," she said. "We're doing just fine without one. Even Robert Lee's shaping up."

"Amazing, isn't it?" said Gramma, smiling. Then she grew serious. "But your mom needs somebody, Cory. Just think. In a few years you'll be in college, then Robert Lee. She'll be alone — and still young. I've been a widow a long time and I wouldn't wish that on anyone. Especially not someone as vital as your mother."

Cory could see the truth in Gramma's words, but it wasn't easy to accept. She liked her life the way it was. She and her mother ran the house and it worked fine. A father might change everything. No way, she thought.

Gramma began singing along with the music. Just to distract me, Cory thought.

"Bloody Mary's chewin' betel nuts, bum, bum, bum," Gramma bellowed. "Bloody Mary's chewin' betel nuts —"

"HELLOO — OO!"

Cory leaped off the couch. "Somebody's at the door, Gramma," she explained, turning off their tape.

"Where's our piggy? She's supposed to answer the door," Gramma said as she followed Cory into the hallway.

"How do you do?" said the person on the other side of the screened door. She was a short, round lady with large glasses and a massive notebook clutched to her front. "My name is Marietta Hunter, and I'd like to speak with Mrs. Dean, please."

"She's not home," Cory said. "She'll be here tomorrow, though. Do you want to leave a message?"

Mrs. Hunter shook her head. "We need to talk. I'm

a member of the Rocky Brook City Council. This is the home that has a pig, isn't it?"

"Yes, why?" Cory felt her throat tighten.

The woman smiled, but it was only a fake, official smile. It made Cory feel worse.

"The city council is responsible for upholding the law, you see —"

Gramma stepped forward. "I believe the police are in charge of upholding the law," she said.

This time the lady didn't pretend to smile. "Are you Mrs. Dean?" she asked.

"I'm her mother. Mrs. Dean will be home tomorrow. We'll tell her you called. Good night." Gramma reached behind Cory for the handle, nudged her out of the way, and shut the door.

"Oh, Gramma, they don't like Pandora! They could take her away! I just know it!"

"Nonsense! There are dogs on this block bigger than Pandora. Somebody's trying to cause trouble, that's all." She stopped, head tilted, listening. "Do you hear water running somewhere?"

Cory listened. Now that the music was off and the nasty lady from the city council had gone, the house was silent. Except for the sound of running water.

"Where's Pandora, Gramma?"

"That's what I asked you when the doorbell rang!"

Cory took the steps two at a time on her way upstairs.

Her feet made squishy sounds on the carpet when she was only halfway up.

"Oh no! Gram-ma!"

Each step was soggier than the one before. The upstairs hall was a small river. Cory splashed through the river to the bathroom.

"Whink!" greeted Pandora. She was sitting under the pouring faucet and on top of the drain. She had fixed her own evening shower.

· Several hours later, four exhausted people and one clean pig sat in the living room. Professor James, sleeves rolled up, was rubbing the pig's back.

"Just leave the carpet out on the line, Amanda," he said. "I'll come and tack it back down in a couple days. It'll take a while to dry out, even in this heat."

Gramma took a sip of her cocktail, her second of the day and a rare thing. She stretched out full length in a chair. In one outflung hand was her glass, barely a foot above the floor.

"It's my fault," she said, sighing. "If I hadn't played that danged music so loud, we'd have heard —"

Slurp!

Gramma jerked upright. "Get your snout out of my drink!"

"Weee," wailed Pandora.

Cory saw that Professor James fought hard to remain polite and dignified. He lost the battle, however, and gave in to helpless, roaring laughter. His whole body shook with it. Tears of joy coursed down the crags of his face.

"Oh, Lordy," he gasped, mopping at the tears. "And to think I've delayed coming over to this house!"

"You can see what you've been missing," said Mrs. Dean.

Pandora the Bold

Over a late breakfast the next morning, Cory's mom asked, "You're sure the bathroom door is shut tight?"

Cory nodded. Gramma swallowed the last of her cereal and said, "Good thing there's no tub on this floor. It's enough that she flushes the toilet every whipstitch."

Mrs. Dean sipped her coffee. "The hall floor and steps look awful now. They'll have to be refinished before we can put the carpet runners back down."

"She is one expensive pig," observed Gramma.

Oh Gramma, be quiet, Cory prayed, afraid her mom was thinking the same thing. She's a good little pig, really.

The good little pig sat by Cory and watched her make a bacon sandwich. Appalling as it was, Pandora loved bacon. She doesn't know it comes from another pig, Cory told herself.

"Mom, what'll we do about the lady from city council?"

"I can't answer that any better now than when you asked me last night," Mrs. Dean said, "but I refuse to worry until I hear what the council is thinking."

Mom, Cory thought, this is one time you should worry.

"She had a great big notebook," added Cory as she slipped a bite of sandwich down to Pandora.

"Don't feed her at the table, honey."

"You weren't supposed to see!"

"I have eyes in my knees." Cory's mom grinned. "And you can't scare *me* with great big notebooks. I see them every day. Also, I don't think any city council can tell people what they can or can't do in their own homes."

"Depends on the zoning laws," Gramma began. "You can't open a dog kennel, I'll bet, or start up a school."

"Oh, pooh, Mother, you know what I mean."

"You need a law on your side," she insisted. "You'd better see what the law says about domestic animals."

"I did that. Cory knows. It says you can keep a dog or a cat as long as it's not declared a public nuisance. It doesn't say a word about pigs."

"Yup," agreed Cory. "And we have to have five acres to keep a horse. That's all it says, Gramma."

"Well, they could declare that pig . . ." Gramma went on, pointing her finger, ". . . they could declare *her* . . . Where is she, anyway?"

She was not in the kitchen.

"Don't worry. She always comes when she's called," Mrs. Dean said. "Pan-dorrraa! Here, Pandora!"

They listened. No little hooves came running.

"Probably gone out for a stroll," Gramma suggested.

"She wouldn't do that!" cried Cory, wishing she believed it. Now that Pandora was older, Cory had trouble predicting what she would do. For sure, Cory thought as she drank her juice, that pig has a mind of her own.

"Soo-eey! Pig, pig, pig! Soo-eey!" Gramma whooped in the traditional, pig-calling style.

"Gramma! She'd never come to that. It's insulting."

"Hmmph! It works for all her relatives. Well, let's hop to it. I don't trust that pig any farther than I can throw her."

Mrs. Dean yawned. "Relax, Mother. We'll find her."

But Pandora wasn't in the house. She wasn't in her pen, either, or in her pool. Three females in flimsy ner nightwear combed every inch of the Deans' ty. No pig.

ng, Mrs. Dean said, "We'll have to search the ood. Everybody get dressed fast."

"Aw, shucks," said Gramma. "I was planning to treat the neighborhood to my shorty nightgown."

Cory jumped into shorts and a T-shirt. Pandora on the loose was bound to mean trouble. And just when the city council was getting nosy. *I wish Mom had thought about her escaping,* Cory fumed. *I can't think of everything!*

She flew out of the house. What if Pandora had gone through the backyard? She could be at Mr. Finnegan's house right now — the same Finnegan who had complained to Dr. Sam. There was a huge garden at his house, perfect for rooting.

I'll bet he griped to the council too, she thought, racing across the grass toward their neighbor's property. She stopped behind the Finnegans' garage and peered around at one half of the backyard. No pig. Zipping to the end of the garage, she peeked out at the other half of their yard.

"Rrrowff! Rrrowff!" An enormous Saint Bernard was charging straight at her.

Fear gave her feet extra speed. She dashed into her shed and slammed its rickety door in the face of the Saint Bernard. "Rrowff! Rrowff! Rrowff!"

Cory pushed against the door, terrified that its old latch would break and snap open. She felt the heavy thump of the dog's body as he threw himself at the door. *He weighs more than I do!* she thought. *If he gets in, I'm dead meat.*

Through the cracks in the wood she saw his massive

head, higher than hers, as he stood and barked at the door. She could even smell his hot, doggy breath. At last, discouraged, he sat down to guard the door. Every few seconds, he barked again.

And then came a low whistle. "Here, Lily. Here, Lily Baby. Come to Daddy." More whistling.

Lily? Baby?? Ha!

With another whistle, the dog gave a happy "woof" and galloped off.

Cory opened the shed door and looked carefully around before stepping outside. Picking at the wood splinters in her hands she thought, so that's Mr. Finnegan's Saint Bernard. And you can keep one of them in the city. Boy, is that dumb!

Sobered by her near escape, Cory ran to the garage. I should have been on this bike right from the start, she thought, pedaling furiously. She circled her own block first, seeing only a few cats and groups of little kids in their wading pools.

When she spotted the mailman, she slowed down. "Have you seen a pig this morning?" she asked, pedaling beside him.

He grinned. "Nope. Saw an elephant, though."

"Thanks," she said, knowing it was hopeless to explain. Then she thought of Andy. Now that Pandora was heavier, Cory couldn't force her to mind, but Andy was just enough bigger and stronger. If Pandora refused to cooperate . . .

Cory swooped up the Shafers' driveway, breathlessly

explained her problem, and asked to use their telephone.

"Be right there," Andy said, slamming the receiver down in her ear.

Cory fidgeted on the sidewalk, peering into yards on either side of the Shafers', till Andy arrived. As they rode along, she told him what Pandora had done to their house the night before and what the city council lady had said.

"If the council says we can't keep her in town," Cory went on gloomily, "she'll have to go to a farm or something. She'd hate that. She thinks she's a person! We've just *got* to find her before the council hears she got loose. They'd never understand. Never!"

"I think the council should just butt out. Anyway, don't worry, I'm real good at finding things," Andy said, smiling at her. Cory wanted desperately to believe him. What a difference a month makes, she thought. I'm counting on *Andy Barton* for help.

Together they widened the search. Every now and then Cory called Pandora's name. No little "whink" answered.

They were pedaling down one of Rocky Brook's main streets when they saw a crowd of people at the ice cream shop. A police car stood by the curb, red light whirling.

"Uh oh, major trouble," Cory said. They dropped their bikes on the edge of the crowd and began pushing through the jostling people.

"Funniest thing I ever saw," an elderly man was saying. "She just butts 'em with her snout, heh, heh, and they're so shocked they drop their cones. Hee, hee! She gobbles 'em up before you can say 'Bob's your uncle!' "

"Yah, hah, hah," chortled his companion. "I'll bet this's the jogging pig we heard about. No wonder she's hungry. Look at her watch that door."

Cory elbowed her way to a cleared space around the doorway and there she was — parked just outside the door. She could have been a faithful hound, waiting for her master to appear. But she wasn't, of course. She was a live pig trap, waiting for the next person with an ice cream cone.

The policeman stood in the front of the crowd, a few feet from Pandora, speaking into his walkie-talkie. As he saw Cory approach he said, "Get back now, young lady! We don't know what this animal will do."

Pandora rose to her feet when she saw Cory. "Whink! Whink!"

"Look out!" screamed a lady in the crowd.

"Run!" hollered someone else.

"WEEEE!" squealed Pandora, scolding the noisy people.

"She wouldn't hurt a fly!" Cory yelled. "She's perfectly tame and I'm taking her home. She's mine!"

Andy called out, "It's true! She's just a pet!"

The crowd grew quiet, digesting this information, as Cory got a grip on Pandora's harness. Pandora looked

up at her, smiled, and sat back down. She turned a hopeful snout to the door and settled in to wait.

"Oh no you don't," Cory muttered. "We're going home. Now GET UP!" She jerked on the harness.

The policeman stepped forward. "Your pig, huh?"

"Yes. We raised her from a baby when her mother died," Cory said, thinking hard and remembering the lady from the city council. It would be brilliant to have a policeman on their side if things got tough.

Cory added loudly, "She's a psychological experiment, really, isn't she, Andy?"

"AT THE UNIVERSITY," Andy said in even louder, firmer tones. "She's never escaped before, see? SHE JUST CAME DOWNTOWN FOR SOME ICE CREAM." Andy flashed his most charming smile. No one could have doubted his word.

People began to chuckle. They edged closer, now that the pig had been declared safe.

"I'll get her her own ice cream," one man volunteered.

"Please don't," Cory said. "I'm sure she's already had some and it's not good for her diet. If we hadn't gone jogging by this store, she'd never have known it was here."

"This pig JOGS TWO MILES A DAY," Andy announced, again at the top of his voice. "She gets weighed every morning, has a bath every night, and knows ALL KINDS OF TRICKS."

Andy turned to Cory. "She should go home now,

don't you think? PROFESSOR DEAN WILL BE CONCERNED."

"Of course," agreed Cory, stifling an urge to giggle.

"Will she ride in a car?" offered the policeman.

"Will she ever!" Cory bent down to Pandora. "We're going bye-bye. Do you want to come?"

Cory turned to the policeman. "Could you just start the car? She knows what a car motor means."

Pandora also knew what "bye-bye" meant. She headed for the street, looking for the car and dragging Cory with her.

The people scurried sideways, making a path to the police car as Pandora advanced. At the car, she looked up at Cory. "Whink!"

The policeman opened the back door and, with Andy's help, Pandora lumbered up over its doorsill and onto the backseat. She pressed her snout against the window, looking out at the crowd.

"You see that? She knew exactly what that kid meant!"

"Yessir, I've seen it all now!"

"Smarter'n that silly poodle we've got!"

The policeman revved his engine and Pandora bounced for joy. "WHEEEENK!" she trumpeted, smiling out at the people as they drove away.

Andy turned from the front seat to grin at Cory in the back beside Pandora. He winked, made an OK sign, and went to work on the policeman.

In his most adult voice Andy said, "Sir, perhaps you

could come inside when we get to Professor Dean's, and Pandora will do tricks for you. A pig is much smarter than a dog or a cat, and tons smarter than a horse. She's been in school this year as part of our science studies."

Cory was wide-eyed. He was a fantastic actor. He should be in their class play and she was going to tell him so. Meanwhile, between giving directions, Andy continued to brag about Pandora for the entire ten blocks.

Three adults, not two, were waiting on the Deans' front porch when they drove up. It was Professor James who ran down the sidewalk to meet the car.

Poop, Cory thought. He could blow this, and after all our careful work on the policeman.

"Are you all right?" he asked Cory as the car drew up at the curb. His hair was even wilder than usual.

Cory leaned around Pandora. "We're fine! Perfect! Pandora just went for a walk on her own." She put her finger to her lips, pointed to him, then put her finger back on her lips and prayed. Any kid would know he was supposed to shut up, she thought, but who knew what an agronomy professor would think.

Professor James drew back, frowning slightly as he ran one hand through his hair. He said nothing as he waited for the policeman to open the rear door. Still silent, he helped Pandora and Cory out.

"Shhh," Cory hissed. "We'll handle it."

Andy hopped out onto the sidewalk. "We can't thank you enough," he said, offering his hand to the policeman. "We could have lost a valuable scientific experiment. Don't you want to come in now and see her do her tricks?"

Mrs. Dean and Gramma joined the group on the sidewalk.

Cory spoke quickly. "This is my mother, Dean Amanda Dean, head of psychology at the university. This pig is her experiment. It's going to be a very famous pig someday, isn't it, Mother?"

Professor James was grinning broadly by this time. He nodded to the policeman. "How do you do. I'm Professor James of the agronomy department and I'm working with Mrs. Dean on this project. We're certainly grateful for your assistance, aren't we, Amanda?"

"Oh, yes," Cory's mother said. "This is a very special pig. I'll just take her in out of the sun now. You know how pigs overheat in summer." She bent down, snapped on Pandora's leash, and pulled her back toward the house.

The policeman excused himself, saying he had to get back on his beat. "You folks try to keep that pig at home, okay?" he said, waving good-bye.

As he drove away, Cory and Andy nodded at one another, thoroughly pleased with themselves.

Professor James put one long arm around both of them and the other around Gramma as they walked toward the porch. "Am I correct in assuming that you two have done a total snow job on that policeman?" he asked, laughter in his voice.

"Yup!" Cory said. "Andy was brilliant!"

"Nice to meet you, Andy. And thanks for the tip-off, Cory. You thought I wouldn't catch on, huh? Thought I was some old fuddy-duddy professor, didn't you?"

Embarrassed that he'd read her mind, Cory said, "Sorry. See, we'd done such a good job on that policeman —"

"And the people, too!" interrupted Andy. "Remember that guy who wanted to buy her ice cream?"

"Ice cream," Professor James repeated, chuckling. "Oh, what a stupendously bright piggy we have."

"But we have a stupendously dumb grandmother," said Gramma. "Will somebody please tell me what's going on?"

Cory waited till they were all on the porch where her mother could hear. She told everything, beginning with the scary part about Mr. Finnegan's dog, Lily Baby.

At the end she said, "And Pandora was just sitting there, waiting till people came out and whamming into them so they'd drop their ice cream. Can you believe that?"

"Yes, ma'am," asserted Gramma. "As one victim of that pig's snout, I believe it."

"I want that Saint Bernard to be confined, and I mean right now," Professor James said.

"Yeah! Right now!" echoed Andy.

Mrs. Dean had Pandora's learning record on her lap. She tapped her pen on it thoughtfully. "Cory, what happened today suggests that Pandora remembered how to find the ice cream shop because you've been going past it regularly, is that right?"

"Every evening lately, but we never stopped."

"She probably didn't set out with that in mind," Mrs. Dean said. "She followed a familiar route and there it was. Isn't that fascinating? How she reacted, I mean."

She turned to Professor James. "Web, doesn't that make sense to you? Just one of those fortuitous things, only she was smart enough to take advantage of it."

So now he's "Web," Cory thought. As in Webfoot or Webworm? Then she was ashamed. He was awfully nice. It occurred to her that he was the only adult to be upset about that scary Saint Bernard.

Professor James stood up. "First things first," he said. "I'll be happy to talk about Pandora later, but right now I'm going to pig-proof this house. You can't have her escaping, Amanda. We were lucky today and we've got great witnesses, thanks to Cory and Andy, but I'd like to make sure our press stays positive.

"After I secure the doors, I'll pay a call on that Finnegan character."

He didn't wait for an answer or for agreement. He jumped down the front steps saying, "I'll pick up some door latches at the hardware store and get my tools. Be right back."

"But I *like* pounding and nailing!" Mrs. Dean called after him. "I can do it!"

Gramma shook her head. "And people think I come here for a vacation."

One Saturday in July

Cory and Andy decided to make Popsicles while Mrs. Dean and the professor were pig-proofing the house. Gramma disappeared into the shower and Cory put Pandora outside in her pool, under the tree.

As Cory slid the Popsicle tray into the freezer, she saw one of those uh-oh looks cross Andy's face.

"Guess what?" he said. "We left our bikes downtown."

"Oh, rats. Well, let's go now while these things freeze." Cory shut the door on the freezer.

Cory and Andy told Mrs. Dean where they were going, and left her and the professor adding double latches to all of the Deans' doors.

"Absolutely nobody is better at escaping than a pig. They all regard it as a challenge," Professor James was saying as they left. He grinned and handed them money. "Here, have some ice cream on me. You earned it."

When they were out on the sidewalk, Cory said, "Boy, what do you bet he's trying to bribe me?"

"Bribe you? Why would he do that? Who is he anyway?"

Cory explained. "Gramma and I think he's in love with Mom," she concluded. "And if he wants to marry her, then he wants *me* to like him too, see? But we don't need a father. We've done fine without one."

Andy shook his head. "I'd hate that. Mom's fine, and she loves me, but Dad's the one I talk to. It'd be awful if he died . . . or . . . or left."

"He won't," she said hastily, sorry she'd brought up the topic of fathers. "Anyway, you just feel like that because you're a boy. Boys always talk to their dads."

"Not just boys," Andy said firmly. "Kids need one parent of each kind — Mom said so." He paused, then glanced briefly at her. When he spoke again, he was looking straight ahead. "Anyway, it's fun having both. Dad teases Mom all the time and she says that's because he loves her."

It took a while for Andy's words to sink in, and when they did, Cory blushed. *He* teased *her* all the time . . . oh, boy, am I ever a dope! Well, guess what, Mom, I am *not* a "natural psychologist."

And again she rounded up all her courage. Andy had said something very special. Now it was her turn.

"Thanks," she said simply. "I didn't know."

"Yeah, I finally figured that out."

They were quiet then, and Cory wondered if she and Andy were now "going out," like some older kids. And what did that mean? Maybe, pretty soon, he would want to kiss her. Cory felt her face grow hot.

"I'm going to try mocha ice cream," she said abruptly, eager for a safe subject.

"Okay, then I'll try pistachio," Andy said. "If I don't like it you can give it to Pandora. I have to go home afterward, though. We mow on Saturdays. Lucky me."

· When Cory returned home, Professor James had left and it was much harder to get into or out of her house. Gramma had to release a stout new hook up high on the screen door before Cory could get into the kitchen.

Lunch — and Hope — were waiting for her. Hope wanted to show Cory the progress she had made on her quilt.

"This's great," said Cory, delighted to see Hope and dying to tell her what Andy had said earlier. Maybe Hope would know more about going out with a boy than she did.

"I thought you had to sit at the Coopers' house on Saturdays," Cory said.

"The Coopers are on vacation, and I'm glad. Their littlest kid, Brian? He's a royal pain. I've been thinking, you know, about my plan to have a lot of kids. If I had one like Brian, one'd be enough."

"Or one like Pandora," Cora said, laughing. She told Hope how Pandora had kept everyone hopping since Friday night. And Mrs. Dean explained what had happened when the professor called on Mr. Finnegan.

"Web decided that he's a very difficult man," she said. "He flatly refused to confine his Saint Bernard. Apparently he views that beast as his protection, since the world is out to steal everything he owns, including what's growing in his garden." She shrugged. "He sounds totally irrational."

"Paranoid," Cory added. "Obviously paranoid."

Her mom nodded. "It sounds that way."

"What is paranoid?" asked Hope.

Gramma grinned at her. "Do you want a full course or a one-hour lecture? And which expert are you addressing?"

"I'll take it," Mrs. Dean volunteered. "Keeping it simple, Hope, paranoia is the belief that the world is out to get you. If you're paranoid, you're exceedingly suspicious or distrustful of other people."

"That sure sounds like Mr. Finnegan," Hope said. "He's a nut case and his dog's a *lot* more dangerous than any pig!"

Mrs. Dean rose, sighing. "We couldn't agree more,

but I'm afraid the city council won't. They don't know a thing about pigs. I'm sure of that."

She put her dishes into the dishwasher. "Can you girls find something to do? I'd love a nap this afternoon."

Gramma popped up from her chair. "We know exactly what to do. We're going to turn the heel of Cory's sock and add a row to Hope's quilt. Then we're doing a rain dance because I heard there's a chance of rain to break this awful heat."

Cory made sure that Pandora was still behaving herself in her pen before they went to the shade of the front porch to sew. There, Hope pulled nearly half a quilt from her giant plastic bag. "You haven't seen it for a while," she said, spreading it out over her lap. "Isn't it great?"

Cory and Gramma admired Hope's tiny, careful stitches. "You're a natural," praised Gramma. "When I get home I'll send you my quilting frame. I'll never use it again, so it might as well live here in Rocky Brook. Amanda likes quilting too, and you all can share it."

Cory looked at her lumpy little sock. She wasn't a "natural" like Hope. She knitted the last few rows leading up to the heel and wished she were reading a book instead.

As Gramma began turning the heel for her, Cory thought, that's my best thing — reading books. How can you make a career out of reading books, for heaven's sake? And I'm sure not going to be a professional diver. Still, the lessons had helped. She could dive headfirst off the low board now without praying that God would save her before she hit the water.

It's a good summer after all, she thought, looking out across their front yard, thinking how much nicer it was to like Andy than to hate him. And why am I worrying about a career, anyhow? Andy isn't. Neither is Hope. I have to just cool it, she told herself. Hang loose, Cory.

She took over the heel-turning when she understood the process, and Gramma got out her own knitting. Gramma finished a sweater or vest or socks every few weeks and either gave her work away or wore it herself. "I hope you want this vest," she said to Cory now. "If I keep it I'll have to move to a bigger townhouse."

As Cory leaped up to kiss Gramma and tell her how much she loved the emerald green vest, she saw a car stop at their curb. The lady from the city council got out.

"She's back!" Cory hissed. "What'll we do?"

"I'll get your mother," Gramma said. "We'll stay right here on the porch where we can hear what they say."

When Mrs. Dean and Mrs. Hunter were seated in the living room, the spies on the porch quietly moved their chairs nearer to the open window.

"Yes," Mrs. Dean was saying, "I'm aware that you called last night when I was out. How may I help you?"

"Well," Mrs. Hunter said, giving that simple word a ponderous significance, "it's about your pig, of course."

The spies frowned at the window.

"Why *of course?*" asked Cory's mother.

There was a brief silence. "Because . . . because a pig in the city is extremely unusual! And there are laws about farm animals in the city."

"I know that," replied Mrs. Dean. "I've examined the zoning code and it says nothing about a pig. I don't know why it would, when you consider how small she is. Mine is a mini-pig, in case you didn't know. She weighs *half* as much as our neighbor's dog."

"Right on," muttered the white-haired spy on the porch.

There was another silence from the living room. Then Mrs. Hunter said, "A mini-pig? I didn't know there was such a thing. In any case," she rushed on, "it's *still a pig* and we have recently revised the zoning code to include pigs. Formerly it referred only to horses, with a mandatory requirement of five acres for a horse in the city. That ruling now applies to a cow or a pig as well. Your property does not meet the requirement."

Cory listened in anger and growing fear. They had made a new law and it was about pigs. Why? Why just now?

". . . will come myself to the city council," her mother was saying. "Our pig is harmless and stays mostly indoors. Moreover, she's a university experiment of some importance. She is no danger to anyone anywhere, unlike my neighbor's Saint Bernard. Only this morning Mr. Finnegan's dog — twice the size of my pig — tried to eat my daughter alive, and I'll be happy to tell the council the facts of that incident. But I'm not getting rid of a perfectly harmless animal because of a new law that you passed *after*, I repeat, *after* the fact!"

The spies on the porch shook their fists.

"The council meets again on the first of August," Mrs. Hunter said. "They'll be interested to hear what you have to say, but I don't think it will make any difference. The law is the law." This was followed by the sound of steps.

The spies bent over their sewing.

Mrs. Dean followed the lady out to the porch and stood there until the car drove away. Hair tousled, face drawn, she turned to the group on the porch. "You heard all that?"

They nodded. "It doesn't look good," observed Gramma. "You forgot to tell her that Pandora hasn't trespassed on anyone's property, but that danged dog was on *our* property!"

"I know, I know." Cory's mom slumped down on the porch railing. "I was still half asleep when I came downstairs, and she made me so stinking mad!"

"I said she was nasty!" cried Cory. "Can they do

that? Make a law about pigs after one's lived here for months?"

"It's not fair," Hope said sadly. "If they knew Pandora they'd never do this."

"Right!" Cory said, clinging to those words. "Hope's right, Mom! Take Pandora when you go to the meeting. Show them how cute she is in her sunglasses — how she comes to her name and flushes the toilet and take her learning record too and —"

"Relax, honey. Don't get all upset." Mrs. Dean stood up and put her arms around Cory. "Pandora's one of the family and we won't give up without a fight. It's partly my fault, too. I should have been more prepared. Web said it might come to this if word got around."

Here he is again, Cory thought. Ol' Webbie. But what could he do? Out loud she asked, "What did he say? Did he have a good idea?" With all her heart, Cory wanted him to solve this problem. She wanted to just enjoy Pandora, the way they all had at first.

Mrs. Dean shook her head. "He said he's working on it. He doesn't want her to go to a farm any more than we do. He and I both believe that an animal raised in a human family will not adjust well to a vastly different life."

She straightened then, tossing her hair back. "Anyhow, we have a reprieve. The council doesn't meet again for over two weeks. And I *will* take Pandora with me when I go. When they see how small she is and how well behaved . . . well, who knows? They can't all be like Mrs. Hunter!"

"And Professor James will work on a good idea," Cory said. She pictured him again in her mind — tall, smiling, with such strength in his face.

"Mom, what is Web's real name?"

"Webster." Her mother smiled. "The whole thing is Noah Webster James, which is impossible, of course."

Impossible, Cory agreed, but she liked it anyway. Especially now. It was a good omen. Someone named Webster ought to be very smart, and they needed somebody smart in the worst way.

"Ooh, feel that breeze," said Gramma. "We're going to get that shower, by George, and without any rain dance."

As the cool air swept across the porch, Cory began to feel better. Hang loose, she reminded herself. And now that it wasn't so hot, she could take Pandora out earlier than usual. Cory always felt good after their run.

"Want to come for a run with me and Pandora?" Cory asked Hope. That way, she thought, I can tell her what Andy said where nobody will hear. "Maybe we'll get rained on," she added with a smile.

"I love that," Hope said, stuffing quilt pieces into

her bag. "Remember how we always played out in the rain in our bathing suits when we were little?"

Cory got the leash from the house and they went out the back door into the yard, where Pandora was in her pen.

But not this time. Along one side of the fence they saw a fair-sized hole. She had gone for another stroll.

・・・・・・・・・・・・・・・・・・・・・・・TWELVE

A University Education

Cory and Hope wheeled by on their bikes as Mrs. Dean and Gramma stood beside the fence, staring at the hole. "Any great ideas, Mom? Should we just blast on down to the ice cream shop?"

"Who knows, honey." Mrs. Dean kicked the fence. "I sunk this fence, too, several inches — just like you're supposed to. Dang it, anyway!"

"This pig is a full-time job," said Gramma. "She needs a professional keeper."

"We haven't had a speck of trouble until lately!" Mrs. Dean said, sounding as if she might cry.

"Not to worry," Cory said, telling herself the same thing. "I've got her leash and we'll find her as fast as we can." When her mother didn't look any cheerier Cory added, "Why don't you call Professor James?"

"I intend to! I did everything he told me when I built this pen and she escaped anyway!"

Now Mom, Cory thought, as she and Hope biked away, it isn't *his* fault. It's Pandora's.

They rode around the block, checking everywhere for signs of a pig. Only partway around, they saw a couple working in the vegetable garden beside their house.

They stopped and Cory called out, "Did you happen to see a little pig this afternoon?"

The man straightened and Cory recognized him as the manager of a small downtown movie theater. "You bet! It was digging up our garden and I chased it off with a broom. Is that the pig I've seen you running with? And aren't you the girl who sold me my manure?"

Cory nodded. "I'm awfully, awfully sorry. She dug out of her pen. It won't ever happen again. We'll fix the pen so she can't get out."

"Good! I kind of hated to chase her off, she seemed so happy, but we can't have her ruining our garden. Good luck finding her," he said, picking up his hoe.

Cory and Hope rode in silence for the rest of the block as the sky darkened and the wind picked up. In the next block a woman was fussing with her birdbath. Cory asked if she had seen a little pig.

"I certainly did! It came right up here on the lawn, trampled all my flowers, and then sat down in my birdbath! Does it belong to you?"

Hope muttered, "A birdbath on the ground is dumb."

"Yes, it's my pig," Cory said, giving the same apology she had offered the man on her own block.

"This had better not happen again!" the woman called out as Cory and Hope pedaled away.

"Did she buy Pandora's Products too?" Hope asked.

"Yup. They love the manure, but they hate the pig."

A few houses farther down, Pandora had invaded a sandbox, rolling in the sand and scaring off three toddlers. She just wanted them to play with her, Cory thought.

In the next block Pandora had stopped to cavort under a sprinkler. "Messed up my front lawn something awful!" the irate homeowner shouted as he replaced bits of sod.

"This is a disaster," Cory moaned to Hope. "She's making enemies all over the place! And she must be really scared by now, with all these people chasing her."

"We could go around tomorrow and give away free bags of Pandora's Products. Kind of an apology, you know?"

Cory tried to smile at Hope. It was a great idea, but right now all she could think of was finding Pandora.

Several blocks later the sound of blaring horns alerted them. At Rocky Brook's busiest intersection, cars were stopped in all directions. "Beep! BEEEEP!" sounded the angry horns of frustrated drivers. No one was going anywhere because a pig sat in the middle of the intersection.

"Pandora!" Cory cried, dropping her bike.

"Be careful!" screamed Hope as Cory dashed out in front of all the cars.

"Oh, Pandora!" Cory dropped to her knees beside her pig and held the terrified animal close.

"Weee," whimpered Pandora. "Weeeee."

Cory was crying as she snapped the leash onto her harness. Pandora needed no urging to follow this time. She raced after Cory across the intersection and up onto a grassy hump under a tree.

Cory collapsed on the ground and Pandora plopped down on her lap. Hope sat beside them and rubbed behind Pandora's ears. Traffic began to move through the intersection again. Several drivers called out or made faces as they went by. Only a few looked sorry for the little group under the tree.

"Come on," Hope said. "You walk her home and I'll take the bikes. A storm's coming and it looks bad."

Only then did Cory see leaves pelting to the ground ahead of their time and feel drops of rain in the wind. She heard thunder and it was close by.

"Let's go, Pandora," she said, standing up.

"Whink!" Pandora set off at a trot, pulling Cory after her.

Hope ran behind them, between the bikes, as lightning crackled overhead. Rain streaked down, soaking them to the skin in seconds.

"I hate lightning!" yelled Hope, her hair plastered to her face and neck.

"WEEE!" squealed Pandora, trotting faster.

Cory tried not to think about the many long blocks ahead — and Hope holding the bikes in an electrical storm. Could bikes act as lightning rods? What if lightning struck one of the bikes?

"Leave the bikes!" Cory yelled over her shoulder. "Put them on somebody's grass. We'll come back later!"

"But mine's brand new!"

Just then a pickup truck clattered along beside them and stopped. The tan truck had a dark brown university seal on its door and a sign reading, "Property of the Department of Agronomy." The driver tore around the front of the truck, yelling. "Drop the bikes! I'll get them! Both of you get in!"

· Later, after they'd cleaned up, Gramma gave Cory and Hope glasses of iced tea and they joined the group at the kitchen table. Mrs. Dean was gripping a mug of coffee. Professor James and Gramma had vodka gimlets. Pandora sat between the people with cocktails.

The professor sipped his and made a face. "Tastes like hair oil. No wonder I drink wine."

"I'll take it," offered Gramma.

Mrs. Dean frowned. "Mother."

Gramma grinned. "Then give it to Pandora."

"Weee?"

All five of them looked at the pig. Professor James shook his head at her. "You need a keeper, little lady."

"Didn't I say that?" yelped Gramma.

"We just can't keep her in the house forever," began Mrs. Dean. "And now the weatherman is saying rain for two days, so we can't even start rebuilding her pen. . . ."

"She's in trouble for blocks," added Cory. "You wouldn't believe how many —"

"I told them what you girls said on the way home," inserted the professor. "They've heard it all."

Slurp!

Gramma jerked nervously and peered at her glass.

The professor chuckled and lifted his own glass off the floor. "I shared it," he said. "She's had a bad day, too, and besides, it might be her last."

Cory froze. "What do you mean, her last?" she quavered.

He spoke quickly. "It's not what you're thinking. No one's going to put an end to her, nothing like that." He leaned toward her. "Do I seem like that sort of person? Is that how you think of me?"

Cory looked at the table, not knowing what to think. She was all stirred up inside. The last two days had been unreal. When she felt brave enough to look at him she said, "I don't know. I just met you yesterday."

"Seems longer somehow," he said, beginning to smile.

"It sure does!" Gramma said. "I've never been so

glad to see anybody in my life as I was last night when we were wading in our upstairs, and then again today when it was lightning and you had that truck."

The professor rumpled his hair, embarrassed, Cory thought — as if he were a little boy the teacher had praised in front of the class.

"Okay," he said, "let's take it from here. Let's have a real meeting and see if we can't work out a solution."

Mrs. Dean sat up straight. "Heck of an idea," she said. "Now, first —"

"Hey!" he said. "Let me be chairman. You get to run meetings all the time. I'm only *assistant* department chair and I hardly ever get to."

Cory's mom grinned. "You're picking on me again."

Yeah, thought Cory, yeah! And she loves it.

"No, just asserting my rights." He turned to Cory and Hope. "I tell you, we modern men are having a time holding our own. You wouldn't believe how the females —"

"High time, too," interrupted Gramma.

"Web, get serious," Mrs. Dean said. "Now what are we going to do?"

Why get serious? Cory wondered. This's a lot more fun. For the first time, she realized that her mother was usually serious. She worked at being a good parent. I guess she has to, Cory thought. There isn't any husband to help her. And I'll bet that's why *I* act older than most kids my age, just being around Mom.

She saw Hope smiling at Professor James and leaning

toward him. Hope sure likes him. I guess I do, too. Anyhow, he and Mom can just take over now. I don't know what to do.

"Okay," he began, "let's each think like a pig. You're Pandora. What's best for you? What would make you happy?"

"Staying here," Cory said promptly.

"Getting married and having a family," said Gramma.

Hope giggled.

Mrs. Dean chewed on a pencil. "Just being around people," she said finally. "I don't think there's any evidence that supports her attachment to one particular person here. She likes everyone. I can't see her adjusting to farm life, I really can't."

The professor nodded. "Then we're agreed that she should be somewhere with people, even if it isn't here."

"Did I say that?" Cory asked in a small voice.

"Well, no, you didn't," he admitted. "If she could stay here we might all be happier. But you see what's beginning to happen that may make that impossible."

"What's beginning to happen?" asked Hope.

"Life is happening," he said. "The normal processes we can't stop or change, much as we'd like to sometimes. Our baby grew up and got smarter. Now she's a teenager, looking for new experiences. Every day she finds out what she can do all by herself — just as all of us did."

He looked at Cory and Hope. "Do you want to spend

every day at home with your mother, do the same old things and see the same old people all the time? Of course not."

"But we're her security. Mom said so."

"That's when she was a baby," Mrs. Dean replied. "But we did our job so well that she feels totally secure now. She has the confidence to move away from us, knowing that we're here."

"Your mom's right," the professor said softly, looking at Cory. "It's the same for all creatures, and the smarter they are, the more they want to try their own wings."

"Ahh. So pigs *can* fly," Gramma said.

Even Cory could laugh at that. But she still wanted to keep Pandora. "Couldn't we fix the pen so she can't get out? She isn't outside much. Mostly she's in the house, and now we're pig-proof!"

He shrugged. "Yes, the house is safe, but the older she gets the less she'll sleep and the more ideas she'll have. She's getting into the refrigerator now and turning on the tub faucet. And while her trip this morning worked out just fine, that only inspired her to try again. This afternoon it wasn't as much fun for anyone." He paused. "You might even say we're all a bit *disgruntled* about that experience."

"That's the worst pun I ever heard," said Cory's mother. But she was laughing anyway, along with the others.

"Something else," Gramma said. "Last week she was

in Robert Lee's bed. Right up there, under the sheet and all, with her head on his pillow."

"Oh, dear," said Cory's mom. "She has the most interesting ideas. I think that's the crux of the problem. She's incredibly bright, and much as I love her, I'm not sure I can keep up with her. It's not as if I could reason with her like a human being."

"And there's the city council," Gramma added.

Cory sighed, seeing the truths laid out before her. "But what can we do? We can't just . . . just send her away!"

"Of course not," Professor James said. "But I think we can send her *back*. My idea is to build a safer outdoor pen so that she can stay here till school starts — say mid-September. She'll be grown up then and ready for a university education."

Mrs. Dean dropped her pencil. "Web! Really? You really think the president will allow it?"

He nodded. "I've been working on him the last couple weeks, ever since you showed me Pandora's learning record. I suspected she'd be a handful pretty soon."

"You mean she'd live at the university?" Cory asked.

"Yes. That's what I meant when I said she wouldn't get any more cocktails. We're not known for that sort of thing at the university.

"You see, she could spend part of her time in the agronomy building and the rest in the psych department. As far as learning experiments with pigs go, we're behind other universities of our size.

"Pandora could be our entry into that field of research. She's obviously a prime candidate, with her brain, and she's a mini-pig, a breed we know less about."

Earnestly he leaned toward Cory. "I know it isn't perfect for you, but you could still make money this summer with your business — until school starts. Then you could see her whenever you want. I'll take you to her myself. Anyway, it's the best I've been able to come up with."

He really cares, Cory thought. He's been thinking about Pandora for a long time. And he's worried about me, too. It isn't an act either. He means it.

She looked down at Pandora, asleep now, her snout resting on Professor James's shoe. It was true, Pandora liked everyone, not just the Dean family.

When Cory spoke, the words hurt. "It'll be okay . . . I guess. It's a lot better than most places she could go. People will be interested in her all the time — teaching her things and playing with her. She'll love that. I'll hate coming home from school when she's gone . . . but that's kind of selfish, isn't it?"

"You're not selfish!" Hope said. "You're very . . . very *grown-up!*"

Poop on grown-up, thought Cory, wanting to cry.

"Very mature," Gramma added.

"I agree," the professor said, standing up. "Okay, then, I'll get to work on that pen. It's just a summer rain out there now and I enjoy that. I grew up working outdoors in all kinds of weather."

He started for the door and turned, "How does pizza sound to you guys? When I finish yanking out that fence I could get pizza for supper."

"With mushrooms," Gramma said.

"And sausage," added Cory. She hadn't had pizza in ages.

"Good. I'll pick up a movie while I'm out. Do you want a comedy or a mystery or a shoot-'em-up?"

"We don't own a VCR, Web. But it was a lovely idea," Mrs. Dean said. "So is the pizza," she added.

He raised his eyebrows. "No VCR?"

"We don't even have color," Cory explained. "We've got this black-and-white antique with a little teensy screen. It's worthless."

His face drooped, making him resemble an over-sized, sorrowful bloodhound. "Geez, Amanda, we had one of those when I was a kid — back in the Dark Ages."

He yanked open the door and grinned wickedly back over his shoulder at Cory. "Tell her she's stunting your growth."

The door banged shut and Mrs. Dean frowned at it. "Somebody get up and hook that top latch, please."

No one moved, but in the silence Hope said softly, "Boy, I wouldn't let him get away."

Gramma nodded and looked at Cory. "What do *you* say?" she asked.

Slowly Cory said, "Hope's right." Gramma was right too, she thought, remembering their talk. Mom needs Noah Webster James. She laughs more when he's here. Me, too.

And I'm right. He will change things, but it'll be okay . . . I think. He isn't bossy or anything, just dependable. Definite. Cory liked that. She always had.

Mind made up, she looked at her mother. "He's a keeper, Mom. Robert Lee'll like him too."

"Well for heaven's sake!" Mrs. Dean said. "Doesn't anyone care what *I* think?"

"No," said Gramma. "We already voted."

"Whink!" Pandora squealed, bumping against the screened door to the backyard.

"Pandora!" Cory yelled, jumping up. "Where do you think you're going?"

About the Author

JOAN CARRIS graduated from Iowa State University and has done graduate work at Drake University. She is an award-winning author of children's books, and has also tutored students in English, French, and SAT preparation. Joan and her husband live in McLean, Virginia. They have three children. *Aunt Morbelia and the Screaming Skulls* and *Just a Little Ham* are both available from Minstrel Books.